SLEEPING BEAUTY'S
DAUGHTERS

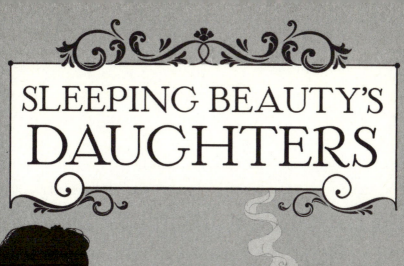

SLEEPING BEAUTY'S
DAUGHTERS

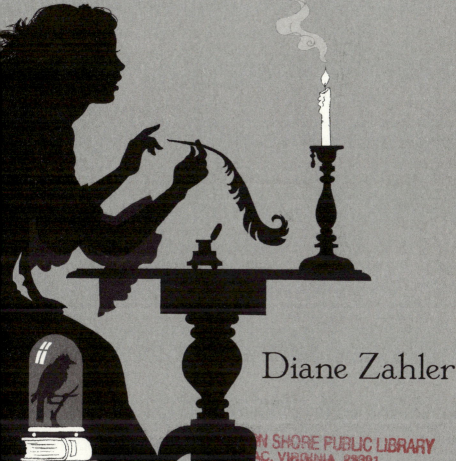

Diane Zahler

HARPER
An Imprint of HarperCollinsPublishers

ISBN 978-0-06-200496-3 (trade bdg.)

Typography by Erin Fitzsimmons
13 14 15 16 17   CG/RRDH   10 9 8 7 6 5 4 3 2 1
❖
First Edition

For Kathy,

who has always been there to pull me from the quicksand

I owe a huge debt of gratitude to my editor, Barbara Lalicki, who has taught me more than she could ever know. Thank you, too, to Andrea Martin, whose excellent ideas have steered me from the rocks more than once. Many thanks to the HarperCollins marketing, publicity, and sales staff—I deeply appreciate your efforts on behalf of my books. And to Laurel Long and Yvonne Gilbert: I can't imagine my books without your beautiful covers and frontispieces. They are perfect.

Cheers to Maria Gomez—it was your title that started it off, and I've always loved it. Thanks, too, to Jennifer Laughran. This one's not yours, but no one would ever guess it from your support and enthusiasm.

For their help and inspiration, I'm truly indebted to Shani Soloff and to my wonderful family. Jan, Stan, Ben, and, as always, Phil—you are readers (and critics) extraordinaire. There's no way I could do it without you.

CONTENTS

Of Honey
and a Haircut

Luna had disappeared again.

I was always amazed at how easily my little sister got away from me. She was my responsibility, and keeping track of her was nearly a full-time job. I had searched the top floors of the palace already and was starting to get worried. If I didn't find her before lunch, Papa would be upset and Mama would be frantic.

I ran down the stone stairs to the kitchen. It was usually deserted at that time of day, but I knew that Luna sometimes crept in when Cook was busy elsewhere and grabbed a leftover slice of cake or bowl of pudding. And my guess was right.

Luna *was* there, but she wasn't eating. Instead, she sat in one of the wooden chairs that lined the long table where the servants took their meals. She was holding out a thick strand of her curly brown hair, pulling so hard it was nearly straight. I realized she had a butter knife in her other hand.

"Luna," I said, "whatever are you doing?"

She turned her head to look at me.

"I'm cutting my hair," she said, lifting the knife.

"Oh no—your pretty curls!" I protested, hurrying around the table to her. "You mustn't!"

"My hair isn't pretty, Aurora," Luna countered. "It's the color of dirt, not blond like yours. And it's always tangled. I am sick to death of it, and I want it gone."

"If you ever used a brush, it wouldn't be tangled," I scolded. "And you can't just chop at it—you'll look dreadful. Ask Madame Claude to show you how to style it." Madame Claude was Mama's hairdresser, skilled at weaving jewels through my hair and piling Mama's fair curls as high as one of Cook's soufflés. But I had to admit that she had never been able to control Luna's wild mane.

Luna scowled. "You know that Madame Claude can't tame my hair with hairpins or combs. If you think I can't cut it well, then you do it!"

At first I shook my head. "Mama won't like it," I warned.

"I don't care. I'll do it alone if you won't help."

If Luna hurt herself, I would be blamed, and Mama would take to her bed in distress. And perhaps if I did as she asked, it wouldn't turn out too badly. I moved behind her, took a handful of her hair in my hand, and brought the knife to it, gently at first and then harder and harder. Luna wrenched away.

"Ouch!" she cried. "Don't pull so hard!"

"Well, this is a butter knife," I said practically. "I don't believe it will cut hair—it will barely cut butter. I think you'll have to pull your hair out by the roots if you want to remove it. And then you'll be bald, like Lord Edouard. Everyone will laugh at you, and you'll never get a husband!" I smiled, to let her know I was teasing. But she wasn't in the mood for a joke.

She grabbed the knife back from me, fuming. "I don't want a husband. I'm not like you, always mooning about marriage and wedding dresses. I want to do things! Instead, we're locked up here. Look at Mama— her life is so dreary. I couldn't bear it if that were my fate!"

"You know Mama isn't well," I reminded her. "She needs peace and quiet. And I don't believe she thinks her life is dreary. *I* don't think it's dreary. She's a queen, after all. You'll marry a prince and be a queen too when you grow up, and I will be queen here. That's important and interesting enough for me." Our parents had no son to inherit the kingdom, so it would be mine someday. Despite my offhand words, the idea had always terrified me. I couldn't imagine being queen and ruling my subjects. How could I face all those strangers, listen to their problems, and dispense wisdom and justice as Papa did?

Ignoring me, Luna got up and moved around the kitchen, opening drawers and cabinets and then slamming them shut in annoyance. "Why are there no real knives in our kitchen?" she demanded. "No pruning shears in the garden shed, no scissors to cut flowers— or hair? Why don't our guards have lances or swords? Why is there nothing sharp in the whole palace?"

"That's how it has always been, and you know it." I was surprised by her intensity. "Maybe Mama and Papa hid all the blades when you were born, fearing the damage you could do with a sharp instrument!"

Frustrated and angry, Luna raised the butter knife and tried to plunge it into the kitchen table, but its dull edge simply scratched the wood, and the knife bounced out of her hand, hitting a jar of honey and knocking it off the table to the floor. The jar shattered on the tiles, splattering honey on walls and floor and even on Luna's skirt. She bent down to grab a large, curved shard of the broken glass.

"Ah! This will do it," she said triumphantly.

"Luna, stop!" I cried in distress. "You know we're not permitted to touch anything sharp!"

She brought the shard, dripping with honey, to her hair and sliced. A curl fell to the ground. I reached out to stop her, but she dodged away, still cutting. I flinched as I saw the glass pierce her finger. She grimaced at the sight of blood, but she didn't stop. Oh, Mama would never forgive me for letting this happen!

Luna sliced through her hair again and again, leaving her locks scattered on the floor as she darted away from me. I chased her around the table, and she laughed and shrieked, overturning chairs and knocking a loaf of bread to the ground. I grabbed for her, but she danced out of my reach. Finally I just stood and watched helplessly as she chopped.

When not a single strand long enough to cut remained, Luna put the shard of glass down on the table. "There," she said. But her voice sounded a little uncertain. Her hands were streaked with honey and the blood that still dripped from her wounded finger. Clumps of hair stuck to her dress. Her gleeful expression began to fade.

"What have you done?" I whispered.

"Yes," Cook said from the doorway, "what on earth have you done now, Princess Luna?"

Cook's broad form filled the door, and her eyes were wide with shock. Her face, usually pink from constant exposure to the steam that rose from cook pots and the heat from the kitchen fires, was now strawberry red with alarm as she took in the chaos of her kitchen, which she always kept spotlessly clean.

"Princess, you're hurt!" she cried, seeing Luna's shorn head and the streaks of blood on her dress. "I'll get your mother."

"No!" Luna and I exclaimed together, exchanging an anxious glance.

"Please, don't bother the queen," I pleaded. "You'll only upset her needlessly. It's nothing—no more than a scratch. We were just . . ." But it was too late. Cook had spun on her heel and was treading heavily down the hallway. I could hear her mounting the stairs, muttering to herself.

"Help me clean this up," Luna begged frantically.

I looked about, dismayed. How had my sister done such damage in so short a time? We could never clean it before our parents came. "Oh, Luna," I said in despair, "we don't have a chance. And Papa will blame me."

I wanted to leave her there to face the consequences

alone, but I couldn't. She took my hand meekly in her sticky hand, and we stood still amid the wreckage. It felt as if we waited for hours, but I'm sure it was really only a few minutes. The sound of boots clattered down the stairs and along the hall, and then our father was in the room.

Papa glanced at me and then stared at Luna with his piercing dark eyes, speechless. Behind him came my mother, her brow creased with worry. She drew up abruptly when she saw the state of the kitchen—the honey smeared about, the hair-littered floor, the broken glass.

Then the smooth skin of Mama's face went as white as parchment. "The blood . . . ," she whispered. Her azure eyes were full of terror, as if she had seen a ghost or a monster. I wanted to tell her that Luna wasn't truly hurt, but I couldn't bring myself to speak. How could a haircut—even one as ragged as my sister's—make her so fearful?

And then, to my horror, Mama put her delicate, bejeweled hand to her chest and gracefully crumpled to the floor.

Of a Story
and a Spell

I screamed when Mama fainted, but Luna just stood there, shorn like a boy, dripping blood and honey. My cry brought the servants running, and then there was a huge commotion.

In a moment Mama's eyes fluttered open. Papa raised her from the floor and helped her to a chair as Cook and Jacquelle, the serving maid, fanned her and offered her water and wine. Mama's dress was ruined, of course, from the sticky honey that oozed everywhere. I crouched beside her chair and took her ice-cold hands.

"Luna's not hurt, Mama," I said swiftly. "It was just

a little cut from the broken glass. You see, it isn't even bleeding anymore." I glared at Luna, and obediently she held out her hand to show the wound.

"And you?" My mother's voice trembled.

"Me? I'm fine!"

"Was . . . was there anyone else here?" The color began to return to Mama's face. She gazed around the kitchen, her eyes wide and frightened.

I was confused. "Anyone else? Why, no. It was just Luna and me. She got it into her head to cut her hair, and I couldn't stop her."

Finally Luna spoke. "I'm sorry, Mama," she said humbly. "I didn't mean to worry you."

Papa's expression darkened at her words. "Why is it, child, that you never mean the trouble you cause? Why would you do such an impulsive, foolish thing?"

Luna swallowed hard, and I felt a bit sorry for her. Papa's anger was rare, but when it came, we all felt its strength.

"I wasn't thinking," she admitted, looking down at the floor. "I was . . . oh, I don't know. I was bored, I suppose. I was so tired of my hair, and of everything. It's always the same here! Nothing ever changes. I wanted something to happen, so I made something happen." She sounded just a little bit proud then, and I frowned at her.

Papa shook his head, his fury gone as quickly as it had come. He could never stay angry with Luna for long. He didn't even punish her after the time she built a fire in the stable to roast chestnuts and very nearly burned it down. If my horse had been harmed, I would never have forgiven her. But Papa pardoned her whenever she cried and apologized and smiled at him through her tears.

"And why did you not stop your sister, Aurora?" Papa asked me.

I gulped. "I tried. I did try."

"She did!" Luna defended me. "She ran after me, but I was faster."

Did Papa's mouth twitch in a smile? "I am not surprised." His voice was stern, but his eyes twinkled at me, and I breathed a sigh of relief.

"Are you feeling stronger, Mama?" I said, chafing her hands to warm them. "Why did you faint? Luna's hair will grow back before long. And Cook can clean the mess."

"Oh, Daughter . . ." Mama's voice was so unexpectedly sad that I felt tears come to my eyes. "It was not her hair. It was the blood—the pierced finger. You do not know. . . ."

"Do not know what?" Luna piped up. "Why should a cut finger frighten you so? What *is* it?"

Mama looked at Papa, and he gazed back at her in silence. There was something strange in the air between them that made my heart beat faster.

"It is time, my dear," Papa finally said gently, and after a moment Mama nodded.

"Time for what?" Luna was wild with curiosity. "Time for *what*?" she asked again. Papa put his finger across his lips, glancing at the servants who were still in the kitchen, sponging the floor and table and walls.

"We will take luncheon in the conservatory," Papa told Cook, helping Mama up from the chair. We followed them out of the kitchen in silence, Luna dancing with eagerness.

"Aurora," Mama said to me when we reached the main floor of the palace, "take your sister up to her bedchamber and help her clean herself. Luna, you will have to bathe—only hot water and lemon soap will get the honey out. Change your dress. Come to us when you are finished." Her voice was stronger now, and uncharacteristically severe. I curtsied to her, pulling Luna into a curtsy too, and we scurried up the stairs.

The upstairs maid, Florine, who was not much older than I, brought hot water to pour into the copper tub in Luna's room. She stared outright at Luna's cropped hair as she prepared the bath.

"Heavens, Princess, you are a sight!" she said

impudently. "You look like a boy in girl's dress. It will take a year or more for your hair to grow back!"

Luna snorted, peeling off her ruined dress and stepping into the steaming bath. "I don't want it to grow back," she declared firmly. "I like it very well just like this."

"Well!" Florine, scandalized, pursed her lips and shook her head. "No prince will come calling for a bald-headed princess!"

As expected, my sister was not displeased with this idea. "That's one problem solved," she noted as Florine hurried from the room. "I said I didn't want to marry a prince—and now no prince will have me."

I scrubbed her hair, rather more roughly than needed, with a sea sponge. "You may change your mind someday," I pointed out, and squeezed the sponge so that water cascaded over her face and into her mouth, quieting her. "You're only nine—you have plenty of time to think about princes."

She shook her head violently, spattering me. "I will not," she retorted with certainty.

I soaped and rinsed, soaped and rinsed her hair. Finally the honey was gone, and Luna stepped out and dried herself, rubbing her head hard with a towel. The hair sprang into tight curls around her head like a little brown cap. Uneven in places, it still was . . .

surprisingly becoming. She did not look like a boy at all, but like a pretty, boyish girl.

"Why," I said, "it looks rather nice!"

Luna pulled on a shift and ran to the mirror. The short curls revealed the heart shape of her face and made her hazel eyes seem much bigger and darker.

"Mama won't faint at this, will she?" she said, smiling at her reflection.

"Well, I don't think she'll be pleased." I was still worried about Mama's swoon. "Princesses don't have short hair."

"This one does," Luna said, turning so she could see her hair in the back.

I took a gown from the wardrobe and held it out. "Put this on, quickly. We must get back to Mama and Papa."

But Luna would not be rushed. "No more combs or brushes! No more braids or ribbons! No more scorched hair from overheated curling irons!" She twirled before the mirror.

"Hurry up," I insisted, tossing the gown to her. "Or I will go and learn whatever secret they are keeping without you!"

Dry and dressed at last, she ran down the stairs and into the conservatory ahead of me. The room was glassed in on all sides and warmed by the sun even on cold days. Flowers and greenery that would not grow outdoors in our windy, bitter climate flourished here. It was Mama's favorite room in the palace, and mine as well.

Mama lay on a chaise in a fresh dress with a cool cloth on her forehead. A small table had been set nearby, and three other chairs were pulled up to it. I sat, tugging Luna down beside me. She tapped her feet anxiously as Papa paced the room, clearly upset. Jacquelle finished ladling soup into our bowls and left us.

Even then Papa did not speak. He sat in his chair and sipped his soup. I had the feeling that he was doing this very deliberately, to punish Luna by making her wait. He would not look at her. Mama, though, motioned Luna to sit beside her on the chaise. She ran her hand over Luna's damp curls.

"It suits you, child," she said. Luna beamed, then jumped up and went back to her seat to start on her soup.

I could hardly believe it. After all the frenzy—the broken glass, the haircut, the mess, and Mama fainting—was Luna merely to be complimented? I had to grit my teeth to keep my anger from showing. I knew there was nothing I could do about it. I wondered, as I often had before, what would have happened if I had been the one to misbehave. But I wouldn't have. I never did.

I pushed down my exasperation and asked, "Mama, what is it? Why did you faint? You are not . . . ill, are you?"

"Oh, no, dearest," Mama replied. "It is nothing like that."

"Then tell us, please!"

Mama sighed deeply and looked at Papa as she had in the kitchen, as if for guidance.

"It is your story, my love." He took her trembling hand in his. "You must tell it."

"Then I shall," she said simply, and she began.

"I have never told you much about my life. It is . . . not a happy story. I was one of two children born to my parents. My brother was very much older than I, handsome and full of life."

Luna dropped her soup spoon with a clatter, and I gaped. Mama had a brother? There'd never been even a hint of any uncle. Why had we never met him?

Mama ignored our astonishment. "My parents adored him, but still they longed for a daughter to pamper and indulge. For many years it seemed their wish would not be granted, so when at last I was born, they were jubilant. All of our relatives, and all the important lords and ladies and dignitaries for many miles around, were invited to my christening. Of course I was an infant, so I do not remember what happened.

But when I was your age, Aurora, my mother told me the story."

Something in her tone made me shiver. I had a feeling that this tale would not end well.

"My brother was beloved by all. Many women fell in love with him. One of them was a distant cousin of my father's, a beautiful woman named Manon. They spent time together, for she was witty and charming, but my brother made her no promises. He was young, and not looking for marriage—or even love—but just for fun. Manon attended the christening party, of course. Nobody knew, then, that she had fairy blood."

Luna's eyes widened at this, but she didn't interrupt.

"Though he was so much older, my brother was devoted to me. Even at the party, with all the guests to attend to, he hovered over me, picking me up whenever I fussed."

Mama hesitated for a moment and then continued. "Manon and my brother danced once or twice, as they had at parties many times before. Now, though, my parents saw clearly that Manon had fallen in love with him. It made them uneasy, and they planned to speak to him about it. But before they could, my brother became captivated by another who had come to the party. Her name was Emmeline, and she was my father's godmother."

"Your grandfather's," Papa corrected her.

"She must have been ancient!" Luna exclaimed.

"She was quite old indeed, but she had fairy blood as well, so her age did not show. My brother turned all his attention to Emmeline. He could look at no one else. They spent the rest of the evening together. They talked and danced and . . . kissed, as my brother held me in his arms."

I could picture the scene perfectly: the two beautiful fairies vying over the handsome prince who held the tiny baby. "Did Manon see them kiss?" I had to know.

"Yes, Manon saw," Mama replied. "My mother said she turned quite pale. Then my brother made everything worse. He held me in one arm and with the other lifted his goblet, saying, 'A toast to my baby sister Rosamond, who is as lovely as the day. To Rosamond, who has brought to me the joy that is Emmeline!'"

"Oh, Manon must have been so mad. What did she do?" Luna asked.

"Nothing at that moment. Everyone laughed and raised their glasses high, and the party whirled on. Later, though, at the end of the celebration, friends and relatives approached my cradle. One at a time, they wished me well. But when Manon reached me, she leaned over me and spoke so all could hear. What she said was so terrible that it made my poor mother faint dead away—just as I did today."

Mama paused again. The room was very quiet; even Luna was still. Papa reached across the table and covered Mama's hand with his, as if to give her strength.

Mama went on in a low voice. "She put a spell on me, a mere babe in swaddling clothes. 'Princess Rosamond, you shall be cursed,' she said. 'When you reach the age of sixteen, you shall prick your finger and die.'"

I gasped in shock, my hand flying up to cover my mouth.

"What a dreadful creature!" Luna cried. Then she paused to think. "But she cannot have been very good at curses, Mama, for here you are, quite alive and well."

Mama smiled weakly. Jacquelle came in to remove our soup dishes and serve the meat, and we pretended to apply ourselves to our food until she departed. When she was gone, Mama laid down her fork and spoke again.

"Everyone was milling about in distress after Manon's pronouncement. In the confusion, my brother and Emmeline stepped forward to my cradle. Emmeline said, 'Princess Rosamond shall not die, but shall only fall into a long sleep. And she shall awaken if a prince with a true heart finds her and claims her with a kiss.'"

"That was you?" I asked Papa. He looked at Mama with an expression of such love that I knew the answer.

"So it did happen!" Luna clapped her hands. "You pricked your finger, and you fell asleep?"

"Yes," Mama replied, "but it did not happen for many years. After the christening and the uproar that followed, the two fairies disappeared. It was not long afterward that my brother disappeared as well." Tears glistened in Mama's eyes. "My parents searched for all three far and wide, but they never found a single sign of them. Oh, but they were devastated!

"Having lost one child, they were terribly afraid of losing me as well. I was closely watched, but I was allowed some friends and went riding and dancing now and then. I also learned practical things—how to spin and weave, though not to sew, for my mother feared needles and pins."

Mama's voice faltered, but she went on. "One day when I was sixteen, my parents were away. They rarely traveled, and when they were gone I missed them very much. I sat in the tower room that afternoon, for I could see the road from its windows, and I wanted to watch for their homecoming. I was spinning silk thread, as I often did, and I pricked my finger on the spindle."

"Oh no," I breathed.

"It happened just as Manon had foretold. I remember staring at the drop of blood as it fell—how long it seemed to take to reach the floor! And then I felt Sleep overwhelm me.

"For a time—I could not say how long—I could still sense the world. A spider wove a web above me. A bird called outside my window. Mice skittered across the floor. But at last Sleep claimed me absolutely. And all in the castle slept with me, falling where they stood."

We were quiet, trying to imagine this. Then I asked, "How—how long did you sleep?"

Mama drew a deep, shaky breath and whispered, "Oh, my dearest daughters, I slumbered for one hundred years."

Of a Tutor
and a Tale's End

At that moment, I heard the crunch of wheels on gravel in the distance. It sounded as if a carriage was coming up the long drive—but we had visitors so seldom. I turned to Papa questioningly, and he blinked, as confused as I.

"Ah, that must be your new tutor, at last!" he said. "I had forgotten completely that he was expected today. Thank goodness—Luna could certainly do with some lessons to keep her out of mischief."

"But—," I started. My mind was still in that tower

room, where a young version of Mama slept. Asleep for a century! It was incredible. And there was something more to the tale, it seemed to me. Mama's uneasiness made that clear. I had to hear the rest.

Mama rose from the chaise. "My head is aching," she said fretfully. "I must lie down for a time. Children, come to my room after you have met the tutor. I will tell you the rest then." She left the conservatory, moving slowly, just as one of the footmen entered.

"Your Majesty," he said, "Master Julien is here."

Luna was on her feet immediately, but I barely heard the footman's words.

"Aurora!" Luna pulled at my arm. "It's the tutor— our new tutor. Come on!"

I shook my head hard to clear it of Mama's strange, terrible story. Yes, our tutor—I remembered now. We had been waiting for him to arrive for days. This would be our fifth—or was it our sixth? We always looked forward to getting to know them, for they were new faces to us, and we rarely met anyone new. But though they came forewarned of our isolated location, each soon decided that teaching rhetoric and Latin to two girls on a remote cliff top far from the nearest town was not to his liking. Our last tutor had left months before. I continued studying on my own, but Luna could not be forced to her books.

We started out of the conservatory. I was slow, still lost in my thoughts, so Luna darted ahead.

"Luna!" Papa called. "Give the tutor a chance to settle in before you begin to torment him!"

She laughed and sped away.

Servants were already unstrapping a great leather trunk from the back of the tutor's carriage when we entered the courtyard, and as I watched, the carriage door opened and a man stepped out. He was disheveled, his clothing wrinkled from travel. He had reddish curls under his floppy velvet cap and a rather long, hooked nose.

Luna stepped in front of him and waited for him to bow, but he only pulled off his cap and nodded his head, as he would to any ordinary female. She bristled, and I could see that she was offended. For all her talk, she liked to be treated as royalty.

"I am the princess Luna," she said in her most imperious voice, and held out her hand to be kissed. Appalled at her rudeness, I started to speak, but Papa shook his head to stop me.

The tutor stepped forward, took Luna's hand in his, and shook it, saying, "And I am Master Julien, your new tutor."

Luna glowered. "Show me some respect, sir. I am a princess!"

He smiled then, and his face became a little more handsome. "Well, I am your elder, Your Highness, and your superior in learning. If you weigh these advantages against your rank, are we not equals, more or less?"

This was so outrageous that it was intriguing. I had to hide a smile as I watched Luna trying to decide what he meant and whether she should be insulted. Then Papa came forward, and Master Julien did sweep him a low bow—naturally, for Papa was king.

"Welcome to Castle Armelle, Master Julien!" Papa said. "We are very glad to have you here at last. The girls badly need improvement." This last, with a smile, was directed at Luna. She scowled when Master Julien laughed.

"I will do my very best, Your Majesty," he replied.

"Princess Luna has introduced herself," Papa went on, "and this is my elder daughter, Princess Aurora."

I nodded my head, and the tutor did the same, saying, "Delighted, Your Highness." Luna snorted. Obviously, this greeting didn't meet with her approval either.

"The queen is indisposed and will meet you at dinner," Papa told him. "We have given you a room on the family's floor, with a view of the sea. Shall I show you there?"

Now I was surprised. Why would a mere tutor be given a room on our floor, and not with the servants?

"Girls," Papa said, "go up to your mother. I will join you there shortly."

Luna began to protest, but I took her arm and pulled her back into the castle. "I want to talk to the tutor!" she cried.

"Don't you want to hear the rest of the story?" I asked as we mounted the stairs.

"What else is there? Mama slept, Papa woke her, and here we are."

"I think there is more," I said.

We knocked gently on Mama's door, and at her soft "Come in," entered the darkened room. She lay on her bed atop the covers, a fresh washcloth on her forehead.

"Oh, Mama, is it bad?" Luna ran over to the bed and took Mama's hand.

"Not so very bad," Mama murmured. Jacquelle had brought her a tea tray, so I poured tea, and we sat quietly beside her and sipped until Papa came in. He took a seat in an armchair by the window.

"The tutor is settled," he told Mama. "He seems very suitable, and looks forward to meeting you this evening."

"His nose is so long a bird could perch on it," Luna said.

"It is not!" I protested.

"Girls!" Mama reprimanded us. "You know better than to comment on others' appearances."

"Aurora says the story isn't finished. Is she right?" Luna demanded.

"Yes, there is more," Papa said. "Rosamond?"

"This part is yours," she said to him. Papa took up the tale, his voice weaving a spell in the dim room.

"While your mother slept, girls, the forest grew up around the castle over the decades until it was entirely hidden. Even the rumors of a castle in the wood faded over time. But then, when I was a young man of twenty, I went riding in the wood alone. I did not often ride by myself, for my friends and I loved to hunt together, but that day something seemed to call out to me. I like to think that it was your mother's heart, ready to waken at last." Mama opened her eyes at that, and tears spilled onto her cheeks. Papa smiled at her from across the room.

"The way grew rougher and rougher, and before long I was lost. I was in a part of the forest I had never seen, overgrown and wild. No birds called there, and strange animals rustled in the thick underbrush. I came to a barrier of vines and thorns. I started to hack my way through them and became like a man possessed. I could not tell you what compelled me to go on.

My hands were soon torn and bleeding, but I could not stop. At last I uncovered a stone wall, where I found a door. I pulled aside roots and briars and forced my way in. I thought I was entering an ancient stable, or a long-deserted farmhouse."

Luna and I sat breathless as Papa continued.

"Oh, children, you would not believe what I saw inside! I was in the great hall of a castle, its marble floor so thick with dust that mice and squirrels had left their tracks all about. I walked past guards drooped over their lances, and a cook facedown in her pastry. My boots kicked up clouds of dust as I tried to wake a servant who had sunk to the floor holding a tea tray. Mice had nibbled away the sugar, but the pot still smelled faintly like tea when I sniffed it. Down in the laundry room, maidservants slept atop piles of folded clothes, and in the hallway even the dogs slumbered with their bones in their mouths. I moved through room after room, all draped in cobwebs, all silent but for the sounds sleepers make. And then I mounted the stairs to the top of the tallest tower, and I found—"

"Mama!" Luna cried.

Papa smiled at her. "Yes, your mother, slumped over her spinning wheel. Ah, even in slumber she was the loveliest young woman I had ever seen! Her golden hair was as bright as sunlight in that dim, musty room. I went to her and raised her head, and I kissed her. And suddenly she woke."

"Why, that means that Mama is a hundred years older than you, Papa!" Luna blurted out. Papa laughed, and even Mama smiled, wiping the tears from her face with a lace-edged handkerchief.

How romantic, and how thrilling it was! I could hardly believe that this incredible tale had been kept from us so long. Why had we never been told?

Of course Luna was first to ask. "Why have you never told us this story? Why is there no talk about it? Surely people must have known."

Papa shrugged. "The servants who woke with your mother did talk, for a time. But who would think it true? Few believed them, and so they gave up, and moved on. The idea of a princess who slept for a hundred years—why, it's the stuff of legends. And so it became a kind of legend. It's a tale told to children in the nursery now, nothing more."

"Well," Luna said brightly, "at least it ended happily, Mama. You woke, you married, you had us."

Mama shook her head in sorrow. "Though your father brought me great joy, it was not entirely a happy wakening," she told us. "Think of it: A hundred years had passed. Everyone I had known, except for the servants who also slept, was dead. Most of the court was traveling with my parents—your grandparents—when the curse took hold. Manon's cruel magic kept my mother and father from ever finding their castle again, and they grew old and died searching for it, while I slept. The world had gone on without me. I had been . . . left behind."

I tried to imagine what that might feel like, but it was too strange. Too terrible.

"And there was something else," Mama continued, her voice quavering. She gazed at me, and I felt a shiver of dread.

"What?" I asked, clasping my hands together.

"We did not have a christening when you were born, Aurora. I was so happy then, and I did not want to tempt fate. But a fortnight after your birth, I took you for an outing in the gardens of your grandfather's palace, where we lived at the time. As I walked the autumn paths, holding you close, I met an old woman who sat at the edge of the fountain in the garden's center. I thought she was a tinker's wife, come to sell baubles, or a pauper, begging for alms. Then, when she pushed back the hood of her cloak, I knew at once, though I had seen her only as a newborn infant, that Manon had returned."

My eyes widened, and my breath caught in my throat. "Why . . . why did she come?" I asked, feeling my mother's fear.

I had to lean in close to hear Mama's anguished

reply. "As she had spoken to me when I was a babe, so she spoke to you, Daughter. She cursed you as you lay dozing in my arms, saying, 'Aurora, like your mother you shall prick your finger and sleep for a hundred years.'"

"Oh, Mama!" I cried in dismay.

Mama reached for my hand and took it in her own. "Manon was not finished," she said, gripping my hand so tightly I flinched. "She pointed to me, as I tried to back away from her, and said, 'But your daughter's sleep shall be solitary. None but she will slumber. No servants, no courtiers, no family will sleep with her. She will sleep on as you live out your life and die. And she will wake entirely alone.'"

Of a Fate
Not Foreseen

Mama could speak no more, so we left her to rest. As we stood outside her door, the hallway swam through my held-back tears. Even Papa's arm around my shoulders didn't give me strength. Luna, though, was thrilled by the story.

"Mama didn't want to make the same mistake her own mother made, did she?" Luna asked. "That's why we live so far from anywhere, and see so few people. It's to keep Aurora out of harm's way."

"Yes, child," Papa affirmed. "Manon never said if her evil spell was to take hold when Aurora was sixteen, as it did your mother, or earlier, or later. So we had to be vigilant. We left my father's castle and spent months trying to find Emmeline to see if she could help, as she'd helped your mother so long before. But she had disappeared completely. We even consulted with other fairies to see what could be done. None had the power to reverse Manon's curse, for her magic had grown and strengthened over the years. I had Castle Armelle built in this remote place to safeguard you, to try to keep the fairy's prophecy from coming true. And to keep Manon from finding us, should she decide to make sure the curse comes to pass."

"And you forbade all things sharp, so Aurora couldn't prick her finger!" Luna exclaimed, and Papa nodded.

"But why have I been subjected to the same rules?" Luna asked. "I was never in any danger. It isn't fair."

"We could not raise you differently," Papa pointed out mildly. "You are both our daughters."

Papa suggested that we stroll along the cliff top, where our palace perched, overlooking the sea. "You need some air, Aurora," he said to me. "You are looking very pale."

It was a fine afternoon; the warm sun sparkled on the waves, though the wind gusted as it always did. We stopped on a promontory that jutted out over the sea.

I breathed in the salty air for courage. Gulls wheeled and called around us, and below us the waves rolled the smooth, round stones on the beach back and forth in a soothing rhythm. Luna picked up shells that the birds had dropped and threw them out over the cliff, laughing as the wind blew them back again.

Still trying to make sense of all that I had heard, I suddenly said, "It was a little foolish to ban sharp objects, wasn't it, Papa? For how could you avoid a thorn from the forest, or a splinter of wood—or a broken glass jar?"

Papa didn't take offense at being called foolish. "We have done our best to protect you girls," he said. "That is why all your needlework is done in Vittray, and why we men go there to have our beards trimmed. That is why we hunt with falcons and not arrows. And that is why our meat comes to us already cut or sliced, and even our forks are dull. But whether it is possible to escape one's fate—that I do not know."

I shook my head in dismay. "How terrible for you and Mama, to be afraid all the time!"

"It has been terrible indeed," Papa allowed. "It was worse for your mother, for she feels responsible for handing down this curse. So it is understandable that she should be quite overwhelmed when she saw the blood—"

"But I was the one who was injured, not Aurora," Luna pointed out.

"It was rather difficult to tell, in all the mess." Papa's tone was scolding and fond at the same time. "And after all these years of worry, your mother did not stop to wonder which of you was injured. She simply thought the prophecy had come to pass."

"But why?" I asked desperately. "Why does Manon hate us so much?"

"She had loved your uncle very deeply, it was clear," Papa said. "And because she lost him to Emmeline at your mother's christening, I believe she felt that her thwarted love was your mother's fault. And then, to see our happiness together . . . In her bitterness, perhaps our joy was too much for her to endure."

I shuddered. "But Papa, what shall I do? How can I be sure to stay safe?"

He pulled me close in a hug, his strong arms a comfort. "We have kept you from harm thus far, my dear. I hope that is some consolation."

After our walk, I trudged to my room. Curled up on my high, soft bed, I thought about Mama's story. Was my curse worse than hers? I thought it was. She, at least, had awakened to a few familiar faces—and to Papa. But I would sleep alone, as my family aged and died without me. When I woke, no one would remember that I'd even existed. It was too dreadful to think about, and I began to cry.

A moment later, Luna pushed my door open and came inside, uninvited. "Whatever is wrong?" she asked me, leaping onto the bed and bouncing energetically.

"Do go away, Luna," I begged. "I'm not in the mood for your games just now."

"Games?" she repeated, affronted. "I'm not playing games. I just wanted to talk about our new tutor. He seems rather . . . interesting, don't you think?"

I turned away.

"What's *wrong* with you?" she persisted. "Do you have a headache, like Mama?"

"You are such an infant!" I flared, sitting up. "How can you be so selfish? You heard what Mama said! Have you forgotten that I'm cursed? At any moment I could prick my finger. I won't know when or where it will happen, but it will surely happen. I'm going to fall down and sleep for a century, and when I wake—if I wake—everyone I know will be dead and gone!"

"Of course I haven't forgotten," Luna said. But I knew that she hadn't really thought about what Mama's story might mean. I closed my eyes and lay back against the pillows as Luna tried to make things better.

"Mama and Papa won't let anything happen to you,"

she said confidently. "They've kept you safe so far, after all."

I thought about how we were sheltered and watched over every day. We had known we must stay close to home, though we hadn't known why. I'd always felt that protecting Luna was my job, but I hadn't realized that my parents did the same for me. They had done so much to safeguard us.

I sat up again, wiping my face with a corner of my satin bedspread.

"You're right," I said, though I didn't truly believe it. "I must rely on Mama and Papa, and you and I can be especially careful as well. We know what to look for now."

"We do?"

I rolled my eyes. "Yes, silly. We must watch for a fairy. She'll probably look like an old woman, as Manon did when she came to Mama. And we must beware of sharp objects. If I don't prick my finger, all may yet be well."

"It shouldn't be so very difficult," Luna said. "You've escaped the curse for all these years already. The fairy has probably forgotten about it."

"Perhaps," I agreed, but just as the dread of the curse had weighed on our parents, so it now weighed on me. Restless, I climbed out of bed and went to sit before the looking glass, taking up my brush.

"Aurora," Luna said.

"Yes?" I replied, trying to focus on my reflection.

"I'll do my very best to protect you—I promise I will."

I turned from the mirror and looked hard and long at my sister. Her face was worried; it was not an expression she wore often. My heart went out to her. She was a terrible pest, but I was suddenly glad to have her near. I smiled, trying to hide my own fear.

"I do believe that you will, Luna!" I said warmly. "Now, let's go downstairs to dinner, and see how short a time it will take you to try the patience of our interesting new tutor."

Of a Curse That Came to Pass

It was as strange that the tutor should eat with us as it was that he should have a bedroom on our floor of the castle. Ordinarily our tutors took their meals in the kitchen with the servants. This evening it was only the family and Master Julien at table. He stood and bowed when Luna and I entered the dining room. I curtsied in return, but Luna, with her usual lack of manners, did not.

Luna was convinced that he was as odd-looking as our last tutor, Master Fabrice, but I didn't find this true at all. Master Fabrice had been a dreadfully disagreeable man. He sucked his teeth with a nasty sound as we worked on our lessons and had almost no patience at all with Luna. Somehow, a few months after he came to us, a ball of pine pitch became entangled in his thinning hair, and he had to go into town to have it all cut off. He never returned. I knew Luna was responsible, but when she tried to boast to me about it, I held up a hand.

"If I don't know, I can't say anything," I advised her, and for once she was quiet.

Our new tutor was quite different. His green eyes were shrewd and intelligent. Luna whispered to me that his nose was as long as Pinocchio's, but I thought it gave character to his face.

"Girls," Papa said as we sat, "Master Julien comes to us highly recommended, for I know his father, King Josselin, quite well."

A prince—and a tutor? I was amazed.

As always, Luna didn't hesitate to blurt out what she was thinking. "*You* are a prince?" she demanded. "Why didn't you tell me that was why you didn't bow? And why are you teaching rather than ruling?"

I winced at her directness, but Master Julien didn't seem to mind.

"I am the seventh of seven sons," he explained as Jacquelle began to serve. "The likelihood that I will ever rule—well, you can imagine how slight it is. And frankly, I would not want it to be otherwise. I have an affinity for books and learning, so I thought to make my way in the world as a teacher. My father greatly values learning, and I have his blessing."

"It is a noble calling," Mama said with approval. She was still pale and drawn from the strains of the day.

"There are few paths open to a seventh son," Master Julien said ruefully. "I am lucky that my abilities and my desire have both pointed me down this one."

"We are lucky to have you!" Papa declared. "Perhaps your love of learning will rub off a bit on Luna, for her grasp of Latin is considerably less than it should be."

Luna rolled her eyes and chanted, "*Amo, amas, amat.* Latin is such a dull language—and dead as well! What's the use of learning it?"

"What is the use?" Master Julien seemed amused. "Why, it's the basis of our language, and it was the language spoken in the greatest empire the world has ever known. To learn Latin is to learn your own history. What could be more useful?"

Unlike Luna, I was quite good at Latin, but I had never thought it especially useful or interesting. Master Julien made it sound almost . . . exciting.

Our dinner passed most pleasantly. Master Julien spoke with ease about every subject that Papa introduced, from falconry to the shipping lanes that led to our kingdom's harbor town. He looked quizzically at the fowl and meat dishes that came to the table already cut, but he said nothing. We parted cheerfully, and I found myself looking forward to the next day's lessons.

In the morning I took a little extra trouble with my dress and hair. Luna, with her sharp eyes, noticed immediately.

"Are you prettying yourself for Master Birdbeak?" she teased. I ignored her, but she persisted. "You don't have to do anything to make him admire you, Aurora. Just gaze at him with your big blue eyes, and twine a strand of your golden hair around your finger, and he'll be love-struck."

"You are impossible!" I exclaimed, putting down my brush. She was almost too much to bear. Why did I have such an exasperating sister? But when she laughed at my vexed expression, I had to laugh too. He was just a tutor, though he was a prince. And no doubt Luna would chase him off quickly. There was no point in primping for him.

We were a little late because of my extra time before the mirror, so we hurried to the sunlit chamber that we called the classroom. I loved it there, though Luna insisted that the smell of chalk dust made her sneeze. To me, there was nothing better on a cold afternoon than curling up in a cozy chair before the fire with a book.

In the room's center was a round table with an inlaid flower pattern in many types and colors of wood. The petals were a rose color that Papa said was ivorywood.

The flower's heart, in the very middle of the table, was made of a glowing golden wood. Sitting at the table, the three of us took turns reading Caesar aloud in Latin, using the most imperial voices we could manage. Luna had so much fun imitating a Roman emperor that she read far better than usual.

Next we practiced oratory, both of us giving the same speech on a ridiculous topic: "That pickled cucumbers are better, both in taste and healthfulness, than unpickled." This was very different from the tedious subjects other tutors had assigned. I was better at speaking in measured tones, but Luna, after she had finished giggling over the idea of talking about pickles, won great praise for her dramatic delivery. She was quite pleased.

"But isn't *what* we say more important than *how* it is said?" I asked, a little irritated at the tutor's admiration of my sister.

"Both are crucial," he explained to me. "If you speak without conviction, your words will have little weight." Then he turned to Luna and went on, "If you become too emotional and stumble over your words, your listeners will not understand you. And if your argument is not sound, they will not be convinced."

Then Master Julien wanted to see examples of our writing, so we pulled out our slates and chalk. The tutor was perplexed. "What are those?" he asked, pointing at our lengths of chalk.

"Have you never seen chalk before?" Luna's tone made it clear what she thought of his ignorance. She rolled her eyes at me; we'd gone through the same explanation with every tutor we'd had.

"The cliffs to our south are made of chalk," I said quickly, trying to make up for her discourtesy. "It makes a fine writing instrument, especially on dark slate." I wrote a few letters to show him.

"I see." Master Julien was intrigued. "When your father engaged me, he told me that you wrote without pens. I wondered how it was done."

He picked up a piece of chalk. After he wrote on the slate, I showed him how to rub it clean. "But how do you write your correspondence? Or do you send slate invitations and announcements to your friends? That would be quite a heavy burden for the post carrier!"

Luna laughed, and I replied, "We don't send many letters. Or any at all, in fact. You can see we are quite . . . isolated here. We rarely entertain. We don't really have any friends."

Master Julien looked astonished, and I could see that he wanted to ask many questions. But he held back, and said only, "Your father has some unusual ideas! Still, if this is what he wants, I can write with chalk myself."

We stopped for lunch, and then spent the afternoon on history and a little mathematics, for Master Julien wanted to see where we were in our studies. Luna surprised him with her ability at calculations. Numbers had always been her strength, while I tended to prefer the liberal arts, especially history and literature.

We dined together again that night, and spent a lovely evening in the conservatory, where I played my newest piece on the pianoforte and sang—quite well, I thought. When darkness fell, Master Julien took us outside and pointed out constellations in the night sky.

"We will study astronomy as well," Master Julien told us, and Luna said, excited, "I've always wanted to learn about the stars!"

The next morning Luna and I came into the classroom early, before Master Julien. I sat down and began to study our day's Latin. A loud thump made me look up from my book to see what Luna was doing.

She had pulled Master Julien's pack off one of the classroom shelves and was already rifling through it, tugging out books, rolled parchments, a peculiar object with beads on a wire. . . .

"Luna!" I said. "Leave that be—it doesn't belong to you!"

But she ignored me, blowing into a flutelike musical instrument that squawked like a crow. Finally, she pulled out a long feather and a little silver container. The feather was striking, an iridescent blue that seemed black until the light hit it. Then it shone a deep indigo.

"What on earth is that for?" I asked, curious despite myself. "Is it part of a nature study? Let me see it."

I put down my Latin text as Luna carried the feather to the table. She stroked it, turning it this way and that in the sunlight that streamed through the long windows. Then she stuck it through her curls, where it dipped dramatically over her eye. Intrigued, I plucked it from her hair to investigate it more closely.

The quill itself was hollow. Of course—it was a quill pen! The silver jar had to be an inkpot. I had heard of quill pens but had never been able to imagine how a feather could hold ink. Now I could see that a little of the ink would be drawn up into the hollow tube, and come out at the point as one wrote. The point—it was so sharp. As sharp as a knife . . .

At that moment Luna too noticed the sharp point and cried out, "No!" Her voice was high with terror. I jumped in alarm as she reached over to grab the pen from me. The quill slipped in my grasp, and its pointed end pierced my finger. I stared, aghast, as a single drop of my crimson blood fell from my hand to the table, where it lay glistening like a ruby in the center of the inlaid wood flower.

Of a Partner
and a Plan

It was only one drop of blood. It seemed so little to do so much. Immediately, though, I felt a wave of sleepiness pass over me. Luna leaped up and lunged across the table, pinching me hard.

"Ouch!" I cried, jerking back into alertness.

"Princess Luna, what are you doing?" Master Julian spoke from the doorway.

Luna turned in a rage to him. "How dare you?" she demanded in a voice so low and controlled that I hardly recognized it. "Remove your disguise, you foul creature. Show yourself to us!"

My mouth dropped open. Master Julien looked

utterly bewildered. He stammered but could not form a sentence. Then another surge of drowsiness hit me, and my eyes closed. Luna pinched me once more.

The tutor looked from one of us to the other like a nervous bird. Finally he managed, "What is wrong, Princesses? What has happened?"

Luna snorted and slapped me smartly on the hand as my shoulders slumped. I straightened quickly. Ignoring Master Julien, she cried, "Sister, the curse has come to pass. You must stay awake. You must! We'll find a way to save you, but you cannot fall asleep. Stand up, we must go. Now!"

Her words seemed to be coming from very far away. I felt so strange. It wasn't like being ordinarily sleepy or even truly exhausted. It was as if Sleep were alive, a being of irresistible fascination who called to me over and over, *Come! Come to me and all will be well!* It was a terrible struggle not to give in. I wanted more than anything to close my eyes, lay down my head, and do as Sleep entreated.

"But I'm so tired," I moaned. "Please let me rest my head on the table for a moment. Just a little nap . . ."

Luna stamped her foot in frustration. "Have you forgotten Mama's story? Your nap will last a hundred years! I'll be in my grave when you wake"—I shuddered to hear it—"and my children will be as well. Stand up, Aurora, now!"

She supported me as I struggled to my feet, wobbling unsteadily. Master Julien stepped forward, and Luna confronted him ferociously.

"Get out of the way, you monster. My father will have your head for this!"

Master Julien protested, "Princess Luna, I swear I have no idea what has happened. Please believe me. If something is wrong with your sister, you must let me help you. I beg you!"

Luna gave my arm an extra pinch and focused her attention on the tutor. "Where did you get the quill pen?" she demanded.

Baffled, he replied, "I always carry a pen with me. Your father said you did not use them, but I brought one for myself." Then he thought for a moment. "No, wait," he said. "I remember now. This pen I purchased in Vittray, on my journey here. I needed a new one—the point on mine was worn down."

"In . . . Vittray? From which shop?" I asked, the words emerging shakily. Vittray was the town nearest our palace, a bustling harbor and the seat of Papa's government. He met with his councilors there and conducted the business of ruling his kingdom in a grand chamber on the town square. I didn't know what shops the town had, for Luna and I had never been permitted to visit. But I had heard from Papa and from the servants that there were businesses of all sorts, selling and buying, sewing and cobbling, baking and brewing.

"I did not buy it in a shop," Master Julien recalled. "It was market day, and there was a stand in the square selling quills and inkpots and parchment. I believe there were stacks of books behind the counter as well." His answer seemed genuine.

"And who was the merchant?" Luna pressed him.

His brow furrowed as he tried to remember. "It was a woman," he said. "I could not tell how old she was. She wore the hood on her cloak up, and her face was in shadow. She sold me the quill and the ink at a good price. I had thought the feather especially fine. I'd never seen one like it before and could not resist. But . . ." He stopped uncertainly.

I looked at Luna, and my lips quivered. "It was Manon, I'm sure of it," I said in a near whisper.

Luna turned back to Master Julien. "That old lady was a fairy, an evil fiend. She tricked you, you foolish man! Unless it is you yourself who is the wicked one, and all this is just a lie."

"It is no falsehood," he replied firmly. "I am not a fairy but a human, a prince, and a teacher. That is all I am." The simple words, and the way he said them, sounded like the truth.

"My sister has been cursed," Luna told him. "If she

falls asleep, she will sleep for a century. We must keep her awake."

Our tutor's eyes widened in disbelief, but then his face began to fade from my sight as my lids lowered. I yawned. I had never in my life felt so tired. Luna pinched me again, and I blinked.

"I will be black and blue from head to foot," I complained woozily.

"We must get her walking!" Luna cried in desperation. She pulled me forward, and I stumbled after her as she forced me to walk the length of the room. Master Julien hurried after us.

"Who put the curse on her, and when?" he demanded.

"Our relative, a fairy named Manon, cursed her just after her birth," Luna answered, dragging me around the table. "I'm sure she sold you the quill. She placed the same curse on our mother."

He gaped at her. "What are you saying? Do you mean that your mother slept for a hundred years?"

Luna nodded, yanking me upward as I tried to sink into a chair.

"Wait." Master Julien stopped by the window to ponder. "There was a story I once heard about a princess enchanted in that way. It was an old tale, and I did not believe it . . . but could that possibly have been your mother?"

"Possibly," Luna said shortly. "The original curse was death, but it was reduced by another fairy, our great-great-great-godmother Emmeline."

I could feel myself slumping against Luna, and she poked me hard. The pain roused me, but it was Luna who let out a sudden gasp.

"That's it!" she cried. "We must find Emmeline and beg her to help us!"

"But . . . ," I began. My thought floated away, but I managed to retrieve it. "But we don't know where she is."

"Perhaps Mama has some idea," Luna said.

"Mama said . . . she said her parents looked for Emmeline. They never found her," I reminded her. "She may not even be alive—it all happened more than a hundred years ago!"

"Fairies are immortal, or nearly so," Master Julien said with certainty. "You must ask the king and queen where to find her."

That idea woke me a bit, and I looked at Luna with alarm. She knew what I was thinking.

"We cannot tell them what has happened," Luna said. "Mama will be overcome. This has been her greatest fear, her most terrible nightmare, since Aurora was born."

"But we must tell them!" Master Julien said. "Surely

they will know what to do."

"No," I protested, my tongue thick in my mouth. "Please, don't force us to tell them. They've spent their whole lives trying to make sure we were safe. If they were to find out . . ." My voice trailed off.

"And they will blame you," Luna added rashly. "Papa will have you arrested. He will put you in the deepest dungeon. He will behead you!"

"Luna, stop," I said faintly. Master Julien paced the room, lost in thought, and Luna followed him, tugging me along behind. My feet kept tangling with each other, but Luna made sure I didn't fall.

Finally the tutor said, "Then you will have to find a way to ask your parents about your godmother as if it were an ordinary conversation. Surely they would not think it strange if you were curious about her."

Luna squeezed my hand tightly and said confidently, "I think they would not. It's worth trying. But can you keep my sister awake until I return?"

"We will keep walking," Master Julien said.

"No more pinching!" I begged, and he smiled at me, though his face was anxious.

"I promise, Princess. Here, take my arm and walk with me. And hurry!" he directed Luna as she transferred my grip to his arm.

"I shall," Luna said, dashing away.

Master Julien and I walked as we waited for her to return—miles, I was sure, around and around the room. My legs felt as if they had weights on them, and my feet dragged on the floor.

"Princess," he said, pulling me upright as I tripped on a rug, "how have you managed with this curse hanging over you all your life?"

My thoughts moved like molasses inside my head. I had to reflect long before I replied. "I . . . I didn't know about it until just the other day. And we grew up . . . we grew up protected. But we didn't know why. It was just the way we lived. We saw nothing strange in it. There were no sharp objects. . . ." Then I forgot what I was saying.

"Ah," Master Julien said. "No knives to cut your meat. No lances for the guards at your gate. No pens—" He broke off.

"No pens," I agreed. "But that . . . that was not your fault."

I couldn't tell how long it was before Luna burst back into the classroom, red-faced and panting. It felt like years had passed, ages of trying to stay awake.

"Mama is almost sure that Emmeline is still alive!" she exclaimed. "But no one knows exactly where she lives. Years ago, there were rumors that she had hidden herself on an island. I had to stop asking, though—Mama got very pale and I was afraid she would faint again. That's all I learned."

"That is rather vague," Master Julien pointed out. "An island in a lake, or the sea? Or in a river, like the Lady of Shalott?"

"The Lady of who?" Luna snapped. "Look around you! Surely it's an island in the sea."

"Luna, you are very ill-mannered," I murmured. "You should remember the Lady of Shalott. She lived in a tower on an island and loved Sir Lancelot, and she was cursed . . . like me." I tried again to sit, but Master Julien pulled me forward.

"Oh, Aurora!" Luna cried frantically. "Master Julien, how shall we keep her awake?"

The tutor stopped walking when he heard the tremor in her voice. "I've had an idea," he said. "Do not despair, Princesses. There is an herb I have read of in my studies that is said to cause sleeplessness. I do not know how long it can be safely used, but it may help while we try to think of something. In the book I read, it was called devil's shrub."

I shook my head. I had never heard of it.

"It is a woody shrub that grows near cliffs. It has dark blue berries. Some may call it touch-me-not."

"Ah," I said. "I know that plant. When Mama is tired and listless, Cook will sometimes brew tea from the roots for her. I believe there is some in the kitchen."

"If Master Julien asks for it, Cook will be less suspicious," Luna said. I had to agree.

"Very well, I'll go," Master Julien said. "I'll tell her I have had a poor night's sleep and need something to revive me. When I come back, we will try to make a plan." He hurried from the room.

The minute he was out of sight, Luna turned to me, her face eager. "Aurora, listen. As soon as you drink the devil's shrub, we must leave."

I blinked. I couldn't imagine what she was talking about.

"We must find Emmeline!" she said. "We will go to the beach and find a boat and sail to her island. We will track her down and make her remove the curse!"

"Why, you are mad!" There were so many parts of her plan that were wild and unworkable that I couldn't think where to start picking it apart.

"Perhaps I am," she replied. "But still, we must try. Otherwise . . ."

I flinched. Otherwise, indeed.

"But how shall we get to the beach?" Sleep pressed on me more heavily every minute. "And what if there is no boat there? We cannot sail a boat. And we don't know where Emmeline's island is. Or—"

"Stop," Luna commanded. "We can't bother about

all that now. We must just go. We'll worry about the rest later."

Her certainty was so powerful that I was swept away by it. Somewhere in my weary mind was the knowledge that I should take care of Luna and keep her from danger, not the other way around. But I had no strength to protest. "What of Mama and Papa?" I asked helplessly.

"We'll leave a note," Luna said. "Hide it, but not too well. That way, when our disappearance is discovered . . ."

"Poor Mama. She will be frantic!" Still, even in my dazed state I could see that Luna was right. I marveled at the way she took charge, when usually she couldn't plan even an instant ahead.

Master Julien came back into the classroom then. He carried a teapot and a single cup on a tray.

"Cook made me some tea, and I removed the vial of devil's shrub when her back was turned," he said, showing us the little glass bottle. Luna took it and passed it to me. I held on to it tightly. The dark powder looked like dirt, but it was my lifeline.

Master Julien poured the tea, and I drank a cupful quickly, burning my tongue. I grimaced at the taste. But the change was immediate. I could feel my back straightening and the color rushing to my cheeks. The fog in my head cleared away almost completely.

"Oh, that's much better!" I exclaimed. Luna clapped her hands, and Master Julien looked relieved.

"I think that I should be the one to try to find Emmeline," our tutor said then. "I will walk to Vittray myself and make inquiries. It would not be a good idea for you to come upon the woman who sold me that pen, but I can ask after her without arousing suspicion. Then, if I find her, perhaps I can force her to tell me where Emmeline's island is. If anyone knows, it would be Manon."

Luna and I exchanged a glance. "Are you certain that is the best plan?" I asked.

"I must do something," Master Julien said. "It is my fault this curse has come to pass—my pen that caused it. I cannot sit by and let you suffer."

"I'm sure you're right. We have no real choice," Luna said. "We'll wait here for your return." I marveled at her coolness.

"Can you keep your sister awake for a few hours while I am gone?" Master Julien asked Luna.

"Of course I can," Luna assured him. "I'll give her more tea. We have the vial of devil's shrub."

"Then I will get my cloak and be off. I will try to be back before nightfall." Master Julien hurried from the room.

"Well," Luna said, looking after him, "if he finds

Manon, she will probably turn him into a fish, or a turnip. For a man of superior learning, he's not all that smart." Then she turned swiftly to me and asked, "Do you know the ladder that leads down to the strand a few miles north of here?"

"Mama and Papa have forbidden us ever to use it," I pointed out. "They say it's unsafe—and besides, it's outside the palace wall."

"Oh, it's not so bad," she said lightly. It was clear from her tone that she had snuck out and tried the ladder herself. For once, I thought, Luna's misbehavior might come in handy.

I said, "Ah well, the old rules don't matter much anymore, do they?"

Luna stared at me. I knew it was as unlikely a statement as she could ever imagine me making, and it pleased me a little to shock her. Then she grinned and replied, "No, they don't. Let us break the rules and descend the perilous steps and find our great-great-great-godmother Emmeline, Sister!"

Of a Desperate Descent

We threw the pen that had pierced my finger onto the fire in the classroom fireplace, where it burned with an unnatural, multicolored flame. Taking up a piece of chalk, I started to write the note for Mama and Papa. It was hard to find the right words. In truth, I knew that it didn't really matter. Our parents would be utterly distraught no matter what I wrote. But I settled on this:

Dearest Mama and Papa,
By now you know we have gone, but please do not be afraid. We

seek Emmeline, for the curse has come true in some small part. I am awake, though, and hope Emmeline can keep me so. I know you will worry, and I am sorry. All will be well.

Your devoted daughter,

Aurora

As I wrote, Luna gathered materials that she thought might be useful on our journey. "We can't go off looking like this," she said, pointing at our elegant satin dresses. "People will know who we are—or at least wonder, and ask. We don't want to draw attention to ourselves, do we?"

"No indeed!" I replied. "But all our dresses are silk or satin or velvet, and finely made."

"I shall steal some clothes from the maids," Luna said nonchalantly.

"Luna!" I reproached her. "We can't steal—it would be wrong!" I felt ridiculous as soon as the words left my mouth. What a prig I was!

Untroubled, Luna said, "I have some coins. I'll leave them as payment. Will that do?"

"I suppose it will." I wondered where she had gotten the coins—but I knew that it was best not to ask.

Luna soon returned from the maids' quarters with her bounty, and she and I hurried to our bedchambers to change, agreeing to meet back in the classroom. I slipped on the coarse gray woolen dress she'd found for me. It was rather itchy and ill-fitting, and I looked frightful in it. It did have pockets, though, which I quite liked. None of my own dresses did, and I had always thought they would be useful for holding a pretty stone found on a walk or a sliver of tart from the kitchen. I slipped the vial of devil's shrub into one of the dress pockets; I wanted to keep it close. Even now I could feel Sleep reaching out from the corner where I had pushed it.

I braided my hair tightly and covered it with a kerchief, so its golden color wouldn't attract attention. Though the day was warm, I put on the servant's cloak Luna had brought me, for I knew the sea breeze could be cold at night.

When Luna reached the classroom in her borrowed outfit, I stared at her in shock. Instead of a maid's garb, she had taken the clothes of one of the smaller manservants. She wore breeches, a tunic, and soft boots. A little cap sat atop her short curls. Now she truly did look like a boy—a very pretty, spirited boy. It was clear that this was her intent, for she laughed at my stunned expression and twirled around.

"I had no idea!" she crowed. "Men are so free—no heavy skirts to pull them down and catch on things, no tight bodices to squeeze the breath from their lungs! I shall dress in breeches from now on!"

I reached out, straightened her cap, and replied, "Ah, but someday you might find those skirts and bodices useful in their own way."

"I doubt that," Luna retorted cheerfully. She handed me a bundle of food she had taken from the kitchen, and then shouldered her pack, which she had stuffed with more clothing and utensils she thought we might use.

"I can carry the pack," I said. "I am older, after all."

"You carry the weight of your enchantment," Luna replied soberly. "That is a heavier burden than mine." Her words surprised me with their thoughtfulness— but they were true, for Sleep pressed down on me like a stone.

I slid the slate with the note I had written under a Latin text on the table, knowing that when our absence was discovered, Mama and Papa would come to the last place we had been—the classroom—to look for us. I was sure they would search everywhere. I didn't want them to discover the note soon enough to follow and stop us, but I did want them to find it.

And then we set out.

Of course it was not as simple as strolling down the drive to the road. We didn't want to be observed, for one thing. The guards at the gate would never let us leave without our parents. And the palace grounds were surrounded by a great stone wall, far taller than any man. The wall started at the cliffs on one side of the palace, made a vast semicircle around it, and ended at the cliffs on the other side. There were acres of land within it, so its presence had never bothered me. In the past, I had never wanted to go farther than the gardens or the small forest it enclosed. Now the wall was a problem, but Luna knew what to do.

"There's a place in the woods where some rocks have come loose," she told me as we strolled through the gardens, our cloak hoods up in case anyone should notice us.

"Papa didn't have that fixed?" I asked, surprised.

"Papa doesn't know it needs fixing," Luna said smugly. "When I saw the stones were loose, I pried them out until there was a hole big enough to slip through. Then I . . . slipped through."

I didn't know whether to scold her or admire her. "And what was on the other side?"

Luna scowled. "Woods, of course. The same woods that are on this side. I was quite disappointed. And then, when I came back, I made certain to replace the stones so that no one could tell they were loose."

I sighed, giving in to admiration. "All right, show me our escape route."

We walked down the hill away from the cliffs and entered the forest, the white birches with their papery bark rustling in the breeze. I thought about the words I had said—*our escape route*. It sounded as if we were in prison, and I saw that it was true. We were very nearly prisoners in our own home, enclosed and entrapped by guards, and high walls, and our parents' anxious love. I had never quite realized it before.

When we reached the wall, my sister pulled away the stones at its base, exposing a hole just big enough to crawl through. The opening appeared menacing to me, but I didn't want Luna to see my fear, so I knelt down and wriggled through.

On the other side, everything looked just the same; Luna was right. But it felt very strange to me, and it was not just that I had never been outside the wall without permission before. The air seemed to have thickened and darkened and grown cooler. I shivered, despite the summer warmth and my cloak, but I said nothing.

"Oh dear," Luna said after she had scrambled through the hole. "Look, the stones are on the other side. Anyone can see how we've gone through here."

I looked at the hole in the wall and the small pile of stones we had left on the other side. Finally I shrugged. "They'll come after us by nightfall anyway," I said. "Does it matter if they know how we got out?"

"I suppose not," Luna replied. "They won't know which direction we've taken. Probably they'll think we've gone to town. But I think we should get as far from the palace as we can, so we won't be stopped."

I started to walk, but Luna quickly said, "Aurora, we have to get to the sea. The cliffs are this way!" She pointed in the opposite direction. I turned and moved toward her, but in a minute I found myself angling off again.

"What on earth are you doing?" Luna demanded.

"I—I don't know," I said uncertainly. "I can't seem to stay in a straight line!"

"Here," Luna offered, "take my arm."

I linked my arm with hers and leaned on her very slightly as we walked. I felt that if I let go of her, I would again head off into the woods away from the cliffs. I kept looking around, wondering what made me feel so odd, but I saw only birds and a hedgehog, and a slow-moving turtle that pulled its limbs into its shell as we passed. Once or twice I thought I felt eyes on us, making the back of my neck prickle, and I turned swiftly. But there was nothing there.

The way was not difficult, for the trees were thick enough to keep much underbrush from growing. We moved due north. To my surprise, Luna was able to tell the direction. "The sun is sinking, and it's on our left, over the sea. Imagine a map. When west is on the left, then north is straight ahead."

"Wherever did you learn that?" I asked her.

"There are a lot of books in the classroom," she pointed out. "They're not all so dull as Latin!"

My weariness and confusion slowed us, and we came to the chalk cliffs a little before sunset. The wind blew harder here, and far below, the waves crashed against the rocky shore. The sea breeze cleared my head, and I realized that I had been walking half-asleep. I drew in a deep breath.

"Are you all right?" Luna asked.

"There was a—a strangeness in the woods," I told her. "Couldn't you feel it?"

She shook her head. "I felt nothing out of the ordinary," she replied. "What was it like?"

"It was cold, and heavy. I felt as if something was pulling at me. I thought for a minute that someone was . . . watching us. But it's better here, by the sea."

"Watching us? Who would be watching us?" Luna turned to look back the way we'd come.

"I don't know. I didn't see anyone. Perhaps it's part of Manon's magic, meant to scare me," I said. Then, despite my anxiety, I yawned.

"We must brew more tea for you." Alarmed, Luna started to search for wood to start a fire.

"Not until we get down to the water," I objected. "If we build a fire there, the wind will blow the smoke away so none can see it."

Luna gave me an approving look and said, "Very smart."

We walked a half mile or so farther along the cliffs until we came to the ladder, attached to the cliff side with rusting bolts. I was appalled to see that many of the steps were rotted, and the bottom rungs were simply gone. It was impossible to tell how far a drop it would be from the last step to the shore below.

"That big storm in February must have pulled it to pieces." Luna paused, looking at the ruined steps. "This won't be easy!"

Peering over the cliff made me nervous. "I don't think this is a good idea."

"What choice do we have?" Luna asked practically. "We must get to the water and find a boat—and we must not be seen. We can't just walk into town."

"But it isn't safe," I said weakly. The thought of climbing over the side and descending a ladder that could tear itself from the cliff at any moment made me feel quite shaky. I tightened my grip on her arm.

"I'll go first," Luna decided. "That way I can catch you at the bottom."

"Catch me?" I said. "I'm much heavier than you—I'll

knock you flat! And who will catch you?"

Luna grinned. "I'm like a cat," she said. "I always land on my feet."

We moved to the head of the ladder, and I let go of Luna's arm. She turned her back to the sea so she could hold the wooden railings and began climbing down. She had to feel with her feet for each step, and I could hear the old wood creaking and groaning above the sound of the waves. But then she moved faster, until she came to the drop-off at the bottom. I peered anxiously over the edge as she lowered herself until she hung by her arms. Her feet dangled above the ground. Then she let go.

"A cat indeed!" I said, relieved, as Luna staggered on the stones below, trying to keep her balance. A moment later I could see her dancing about with glee.

"It's fun, Sister!" she called, the wind snatching at her words.

I stood at the top of the ladder and turned. Gripping the railings so hard that I could feel splinters from the rotted wood piercing my skin, I put one foot on the top step. There! Step by step I inched my way downward. When my foot reached the fifth rung, it creaked and tilted, but I held on so tightly that I didn't slip.

I don't know whether it was because I was slower than Luna, or because I was heavier, or both. But when a sudden gust of wind shook the ladder, it gave a great rasping groan and began to break away from the cliff. Above me I could see each step swing free, one by one. The fourth step, the third, the second . . . When the top step broke loose I would plunge with the ladder to the rocks below. I cried out in terror and closed my eyes as I began to fall. It seemed to happen slowly, so that falling felt almost as I imagined flying might feel. And I had time to think to myself, most regretfully, *Oh, if only I had known I was to die like this, I wouldn't have struggled so hard against Sleep!*

Of a Sailor
and a Storm Cloud

I heard Luna scream as I tumbled down. Then, all at once, I jerked to a stop. I felt a firm grasp around my waist, like arms holding me up. I opened my eyes and saw the rocky beach below, where Luna stood gazing at me. Above me was the cliff. I floated in the air between the two, my skirts waving in the wind.

"Aurora!" Luna shouted. Leaping up as high as she could, she grabbed the bottom of my skirt and yanked me downward. As if something suddenly let me go, I fell to the ground.

After a moment Luna helped me to stand, and we gazed up at the cliff. A ray of sun pierced the thin clouds, which were tinged pink by the sunset. In the rosy light a figure gradually became visible. It hovered in the air, wavering and indistinct at first, then growing clearer. I could make out the shape of a man, a handsome face, a mouth open and laughing. Then, as the clouds covered the sun's ray again, the form disappeared.

We were completely speechless.

"You there!" a voice cried, startling us. "Are you all right?"

I turned to see a boy rushing toward us, moving nimbly among the rocks. He was about my age or a little older, dressed in a patched and shapeless wool tunic. He had long, sun-streaked hair and wore an old knitted cap.

He drew up to us, panting, and asked again, "Are you all right? I saw the ladder fall, and then—" He broke off and pointed at the spot where we'd seen the apparition.

"You are surpassingly lucky, miss," he said to me. "If that lutin had not been near—well, I hate to think of what would have happened to you!"

"A lutin? What on earth is a lutin?" Luna demanded.

"Why, it's an imp," the boy replied, as if she were an idiot for not knowing. "Have you never heard of lutins?"

Luna shook her head, but I remembered reading about them. "I thought they were only in folk stories," I said. "Are they real? Are you sure?"

"Aye, miss, they're real enough," the boy said. "Lucky for you! They can fly through the air without wings and swim through the water without gills, and enter through closed doors and windows." He grinned, a funny, lopsided grin. "They're immortal, and invisible as well, when they wish to be."

Luna was intrigued. "But are they good or wicked?"

The boy shrugged. "Neither—or both," he replied. "I think they act as they please. I've heard of one who saved a maiden from robbers, and another who nailed a man to a wall by the ear."

"Oh my," I said faintly. "This one, I suppose, was good, for he surely saved me. If he hadn't caught me . . ." Then I wobbled a bit, and Luna took my arm.

"We must build a fire and brew the tea," she said urgently.

The boy looked surprised, but he said, "I have a fire lighted close by, and I was just going to cook some fish I'd caught." He pointed to a sack that he'd dropped onto the sand when he ran toward us. "I can make tea as well. Will you eat with me?"

"We would be thankful to share your fire and your catch," I said gratefully. The boy slung the sack over his shoulder, and we started down the strand together.

"I'm Symon," the boy said as he walked sure-footedly among the rocks. "I'm a fisherman by trade."

"My nose tells me that," Luna murmured under her breath. I was too shaken and tired to scold her.

Stumbling after him, I said, "I am Aurora, and this is—" I broke off as Luna interrupted me.

"I am her brother Louis," she said firmly, touching the cap on her cropped hair.

"Glad to make your acquaintance," Symon told us. A moment later we reached a small opening in the cliff side. "Welcome to my humble abode," he said, bowing as he motioned us inside. We ducked into the cave. It was damp but cozy, with a banked fire that Symon quickly coaxed to a warming blaze. Before the fire Symon had placed an old rag rug so he would not have to sit on the cold sand. A few cook pots and dishes were piled nearby.

At Luna's urging, Symon pulled out a pot from the pile, filled it with fresh water that he had collected in a jar, and positioned it over the flames. The water boiled in a few minutes, and I sprinkled the devil's shrub powder on top, brewing the tea. Then I drank deeply. Again I felt restored, and energy coursed through me. Symon watched without speaking, his eyes sharp and curious.

Then he said, "Supper!" and pulled a string of silver fish from the sack and a pan from the pile of cookware. We sat cross-legged on the rug and watched as he fried up a surprisingly tasty meal. We added bread and cheese from the food Luna had taken from the palace kitchen and ate every bite, burning our fingers on the crispy fish, for Symon had no forks. It was a fine feast, and we felt much better for it.

"That was not at all bad," Luna said, patting her stomach, "though I'm sorry there's no sweet."

The boy burst out laughing. "Why, I'll just bake you up a dessert, sir!" he said. "Would you like a cod pudding, or a sea bass tart?"

"There is no need to be rude," Luna snapped, making him laugh again. She got up and stomped out of the cave, furious, and Symon looked quizzically at me.

"My . . . brother has a quick temper," I explained. "He'll be over it soon." Symon raised an eyebrow, and I wondered if Luna's disguise had entirely fooled him.

In fact, Luna was back again quite quickly, for the evening wind was chill. She sat close to the fire and listened as Symon explained why he fished alone.

"I'm an orphan," he said matter-of-factly. "My father was a fisherman, and his father before him—as far back as any can remember. Father perished in the sea when I was just six, and I took up his nets and his boat as soon as I could. I caught enough to keep my mother and myself in food and clothing." He paused for a moment. "This past winter Mother fell ill with ship fever and died. And so I fend for myself now."

His voice was calm, though he described dreadful losses. I thought of Mama, so weak and delicate. I too could lose my mother. The terror she must be feeling over our disappearance could kill her. The idea made tears spring to my eyes.

"It's not right, that you should have to live alone, and work so much!" I said, blinking hard.

"It's the way it is," Symon replied. "I love the sea. And there are those who watch out for me."

"Who?" Luna asked, her anger forgotten.

Symon gave her a quick smile. "The fishermen of Vittray are kind, and are always willing to help me mend my torn nets. Their wives often have a loaf of bread or a pigeon pie extra. I do quite well."

"Do you live in this cave? Do you not go to school?" I inquired.

"Oh, how wonderful!" Luna exclaimed. To live in a cave and not take lessons—that was her idea of bliss. But Symon shook his head.

"I stay here when the fish are running. I can reach them more easily—and earlier than the other fisher-men—if I leave from this strand rather than the harbor.

But I have a home in Vittray, my mother's cottage. And though I don't go to school anymore, I read. I learn from books. At home I have many, for my mother's father was a schoolteacher. I love to read about the sea." He closed his eyes and recited,

"A life on the ocean wave,
A home on the rolling deep,
Where the scattered waters rave,
And the winds their revels keep!"

Luna and I applauded. I knew a few sea poems myself, from the days when one of our tutors, Master Orland, had forced us to recite long verses every week. So I boldly replied,

"Who hath desired the Sea?—the sight of salt water unbounded—
The heave and the halt and the hurl and the crash of the comber wind-hounded?"

And back again Symon rejoined,

"I must down to the seas again, for the call of the running tide
Is a wild call and a clear call that may not be denied!"

We burst out laughing, very pleased with ourselves. "I think I should like a life on the sea," Luna said softly, tracing a pattern in the sand with her finger.

"But what of the fish smell?" I reminded her.

"Oh, I could get used to it, I'm sure," she said.

"Well then, lad," Symon told her, "you shall be my apprentice, and I will teach you to sail and fish!"

Luna caught my eye, and we smiled. I imagined her in her velvets and silks pulling in a net full of flapping, briny fish. What a mess she would be!

"But you two," Symon said then, "what are you doing on the strand, a mile or more from Vittray harbor?"

We were silent for a moment, wondering how much to tell him. Finally I spoke. "We are on a kind of quest," I said carefully. "My brother and I seek a relative of ours, a woman who lives on an island."

"Why do you seek her?" Symon asked. It was a reasonable question, but of course we did not have a reasonable answer.

"Someone in our family is . . . ill, and our relative is the only one who can cure her." I took a deep breath. "She is a fairy."

"I see," Symon said thoughtfully. "And where is the island?"

"We don't know." His eyes widened in surprise. "We only know she lives on an island."

Symon considered this. "I don't go out very far, for I have only a small boat—a batteau," he said. "But I've heard tell of islands a few leagues to the north. I should be glad to take you, if my little craft can do it."

"Oh, would you? Really?" I clasped my hands together. "I didn't want to ask—but we don't know how to sail, and we have no boat. It would be so kind of you! We could pay you well."

Symon's brows went up. I suppose we didn't look as if we had much money in the pockets of our servants' clothes. But he nodded and grinned his funny grin. "Then we all would benefit," he said. "If the weather holds fine, we can leave at dawn."

The night drew in, and we arranged ourselves as comfortably as we could around the fire. Luna and I had a whispered conference and decided that to keep me awake during the night, she would sleep a short while, until the devil's shrub began to wear off. Then I would have more tea, and she would wake to help me stay up.

As the fire crackled, and Luna curled up on the rug beside me, Symon told a tale of the most renowned of the lutins, Leander. Long ago he had been a human prince, and an evil enchantress had hunted him, determined to destroy him.

"No one knew why the enchantress hated Leander so, but she was relentless. She followed him to the ends of the earth and trapped him in a deep cavern. For years he suffered there, waiting for the terrible end the enchantress had threatened him with. She came to him now and then, but she didn't kill him, though in his loneliness and despair he longed for death.

"At last a beautiful fairy found Leander in his secret prison. She offered to change him into a lutin so he could escape. And Leander said yes."

"So he was an imp, then?" I asked. "Aren't they supposed to be little and funny-looking?"

"Lutins are a little different, I've heard. They look human because they once were human, but they've an imp's powers."

"Do you think Leander is the one who saved Aurora?" Luna asked sleepily.

"It could be," Symon replied. "Leander is known for helping maidens in distress."

I thought of the peculiar feeling of hanging in the air, with only invisible arms to support me. "I am very lucky, I suppose," I said softly. But I did not feel lucky.

"We should sleep," Symon said then, lying back and pulling his cloak over himself like a blanket. I covered Luna, already asleep, with her cloak.

The minutes passed with painful slowness as I tried to keep my eyes from closing. The waves broke against the shore in a muted, regular rhythm like the breath of the sea, and the fire's warmth was like my mother's arms, urging me to sleep. I dug my nails into my palms, got up, and danced around. I played a quiet game with myself, finding animal shapes on the cave wall made by the firelight's flickering shadows. I held off making more tea as long as I dared, for the vial that held the devil's shrub powder was very small, and I didn't want to run out. Finally, though, I had to brew and drink a cupful. Then I shook Luna. She had always been a hard sleeper, and she muttered and protested and did not wake.

"What is it?" Symon whispered. "Can you not sleep?"

I looked at his kind face in the dancing firelight. "I dare not," I said simply.

He didn't ask more. "I will stay up with you," he said, pushing aside his cloak.

"No, you needn't," I protested. He ignored me.

"We can tell stories," he said. "There are many seafaring tales in the books I've read, if you care to hear them."

"Oh, I would like that!" I exclaimed. So he told me the tale of a crazed sea captain who hunted a white whale that had bitten off his leg, until the whale took down his ship and him with it. Then he related the story of the ship's crew that mutinied against a dreadful captain and were stranded on a strange island for years. And I told him the tale of the mariner Odysseus, who, on his way home from the Trojan War, had ten years of adventures before he could be reunited with his wife.

The glow of dawn appeared, turning the sand a pale peach color between the dark stones. Luna woke, cranky and hugely annoyed that we had spent the night in storytelling without her, but I hushed her complaints.

"You're lucky you slept," I told her. "You'll be in charge of keeping us awake today." She liked the responsibility of that and stopped grumbling.

We ate a quick meal of bread and cheese, and I had my tea, relieved to be alert again. Then we prepared Symon's vessel for the journey.

It was a funny little boat, the batteau, flat-bottomed with a high prow. A weather-beaten script on the side read *Cateline*. "My mother's name," Symon said gruffly.

"It's a very beautiful name," I told him, and he smiled at me gratefully.

A short mast stuck up from the center of the boat like an afterthought, and from it Symon raised a small sail. Two benches were in front of the mast.

"Louis," Symon said to Luna, but she didn't respond. "Louis!" he repeated, and Luna remembered all at once that she was my brother now, not my sister.

"Yes?" she replied, pitching her voice lower than usual.

Symon exchanged a glance with me, smiling. "You take the front-most seat, in the bow. Aurora, you can sit on the second bench. From there you can tend the sail."

Symon gave me some brief instruction on how to manage the ropes, warning that the boom—the heavy wooden piece at the bottom of the sail—would swing around when the boat turned. I would have to duck to avoid being hit on the head.

"Usually," Symon said, "I can man the sail and the tiller both. But we'll be going out farther than I've gone before, and we may be sailing for more than a day. I'll need help."

"I can tend the sail," Luna said indignantly. "Why don't I sit there instead of Aurora?"

I didn't think she would have either the strength or the patience to work the sail, but I didn't want to say so. "Your sight is so keen," I pointed out. "If you're in the front, you can be the lookout. I am sure you'd see land before either of us."

Luna frowned, but she had to admit this was true. She had the eyes of a hawk. She once saw a whale far out at sea from our palace on the cliff, and she always noticed when a servant had left a spot undusted or pocketed a silver spoon. She took her place in the bow.

Symon took the small bench nearest the back—the stern—so he could steer the boat with the tiller. There were nets piled in the bottom; Symon shoved them beneath the benches as we pushed the boat into the waves and climbed in. Our shoes and legs were soaked.

"Oh, it stinks!" Luna cried. Though I hushed her, she was quite right. It was fishy in the extreme. The bottom was slippery with scales.

Luna found a fish eyeball among the scales and held it up. "The fish are watching us," she said with glee. "Fish spies are everywhere!"

I knew she was joking, but the idea of spies gave me pause. I thought of the way I had felt in the forest, how I had kept looking around to see if anyone was watching us. To keep that uncomfortable thought away, I reached forward and batted the eyeball out of Luna's hand. It flew through the air and landed on my skirt. Despite myself I shrieked and jumped up, rocking our little vessel wildly.

"Sit down!" Symon commanded in a stern voice, pointing to the wooden benches. "The first rule in the *Cateline* is this: Never stand up! It is a hardy boat, and a sturdy one, but if you rock it enough it will tip, and the water is chill even in summer."

"I love a good swim," Luna said offhandedly, and I frowned at her, for she could no more swim than fly through the air. But she added, "Yes sir, Captain!" We kept up calling Symon Captain, as he seemed to like it, and Luna quickly claimed the title of First Mate. The only position left for me was Deckhand. This pleased Luna enormously, as it sounded lowly and undignified, but I accepted the title with good grace, sure that I would never actually have to swab the decks on our short journey.

As we sailed, all we saw was water and more water, with an occasional glimpse of gull or tern or pelican bobbing on the waves. The wind was stiff, and we skimmed along with little effort. It was wonderfully pleasant: The sun was bright, the air cool, the spray from the water invigorating. Sleep seemed far away. Every once in a while Symon would call out, "Haul the sheets!" and I would pull on the ropes until the sail was taut in the wind.

I noticed, though, that with each slap of the waves against the sides of the boat, Luna grew paler. Before long she was a dreadful greenish hue, and Symon took note.

"Louis, are you seasick?" he asked. His tone was sympathetic, but Luna bristled.

"Of course I'm not!" she retorted. "I'm a little tired, that's all. I didn't sleep well. And there is the smell of fish—" She suddenly clapped a hand over her mouth.

"Downwind!" Symon commanded, pointing to the stern of the boat. Luna scrambled over the bench beside me, around the mast, and stopped at Symon's bench, rocking the little craft. She deposited her breakfast into the sea. Then she collapsed on the bottom of the boat, groaning.

"Oh no!" I cried, reaching out for her. "What's wrong? Should we go back and find a doctor?"

"Go back?" Symon scoffed. "For seasickness? He'll get his sea legs before long. Besides, I thought your fairy relative was a healer of some sort. Isn't that why you're trying to find her? I'm sure if anything truly ails Louis, your relative will make it better."

"I'm fine," Luna said, getting up and crawling back to her place. Indeed, a little color had returned to her cheeks, so I held my tongue, and we went on.

We sailed until the sun was nearly straight overhead. Once, far off, I noticed something that looked like a little trail of smoke rising from the water. "A whale, spouting," Symon said. "That's how they breathe."

And then, suddenly, I saw a massive, towering shape on the horizon. I was certain that a moment before there had been nothing there.

Luna saw it at the same moment. "Land ho! Is it an island?" she called out.

Symon peered into the distance, and then shook his head slowly. "I think not," he replied in a worried tone. "I believe it's a storm cloud—though I've never seen one like it."

Storm clouds often shrouded our castle on the cliffs, but they didn't look like this. The cloud seemed to mount to the very heavens, and lightning flashed deep within its purplish billows. It moved toward us with astonishing speed. A great howling wind came before it, catching Symon unprepared. It propelled us backward so quickly that we nearly overturned, the boat heeling until waves splashed over the side.

"Strike sail!" Symon cried. I had no idea what the command meant, though, and the wind was too strong for me to respond even if I had known. Ripping free of the mast, the sail flew off like a huge white kite. The boom swung around violently, just missing me as I ducked. Then we were at the wind's mercy.

"Row!" shouted Symon, straining at the tiller. There were long wooden oars on each side of the boat. I grabbed for the starboard oar near me and tried to work it through the water, while Luna did the same on the other side. The oars were useless, though, against the power of that wind.

Thunder cracked, and lightning played in the dark cloud that now hung directly above us. Rain began to fall, pounding down so hard it actually hurt. We were soaked to the skin in an instant. The waves were enormous, whipped into a frenzy by the wind. The *Cateline* quickly began to fill with water from both above and below.

"Bail!" Symon yelled. I could barely hear him now over the howl of the gale. I dropped my useless oar and found a wooden bucket beneath the seat. Though I worked as fast as I could, I was nearly blinded by the raging storm. I couldn't begin to keep up with the water that poured into the boat.

The batteau climbed each wave and then rushed into its trough, leaving our stomachs at the top as the next wave rose up behind us. Symon had managed to turn the boat around, so we were hurtling back toward land. We sped up and down the mountainous waves as if in a race for our very lives. The violent movement made me as seasick as Luna had been, but I was so frantic to bail that I would not give in to my queasiness.

By the time the shore came into view, the boat was filled with water and we were riding very low. My arms trembled with exhaustion, but I kept bailing and saw that Luna had found another bucket and was doing the same. It was clear that we were not approaching the strand where we had stayed the night; I could see the red-tiled roofs of many buildings as we swiftly drew closer. We were speeding straight into the harbor of Vittray, its waters dotted with anchored trading ships.

The ships' crews stood on the decks and watched in astonishment as we whipped past them. Their open mouths and pointing hands were a blur to me. With the gale at our backs, we sped through the harbor as if hurled by an unseen hand. Symon struggled with the tiller, and somehow we avoided the vessels, big and small, rocking on their tethers.

On we raced, using the oars to try to keep us from colliding with one boat and then another. Then I saw the great pier of Vittray, which stuck out a hundred yards into the harbor. It seemed that we would surely hit it—we must hit it!—but I had forgotten how very small the batteau was, and how low it rode. Instead, as we whooshed under the pier, the mast struck it and broke off with a great *crack*. And with one last thrust, the wind heaved the *Cateline* onto the sandy beach beneath the pier. The sudden stop flung all three of us—Captain, First Mate, and Deckhand—out of the boat and into a sodden heap on the shore.

9

Of a Refuge
and a Route

L anding on the hard sand knocked the air right out of me. There was a horrible moment when I couldn't breathe and was sure I never would breathe again, and then a sudden, painful gasp as I inhaled. As soon as my lungs filled, I spat out a mouthful of sand.

I heard Luna bellow, "Get that elbow out of my ear!" Thank goodness she was all right. I was pretty certain it was my elbow she meant, but I could barely move. Finally I pushed at the bodies atop me and struggled out of the wet pile on hands and knees, stopping only when I saw a circle of feet at my eye level. We were surrounded.

I lifted my gaze past ankles, shins, and waists fat and skinny, to the startled faces of the people of Vittray. They gaped at us in amazement. I could see why—it must have looked like an invisible hand had pushed us beneath the pier in our little boat and tumbled us out onto the sand. What a tale for fishermen and boat builders to tell by their firesides! But the stares made me aware of what a mess I was, and I began to feel very awkward and uncomfortable.

We got stiffly to our feet, trying to brush the sand off our soaked clothes. "Well, what are you staring at?" Luna challenged the shocked faces around us. "Have you never seen shipwreck victims before?"

A woman with iron-gray hair and broad red cheeks stepped forward. "Child," she exclaimed, "you were lucky you weren't all killed!"

A rough-looking man beside her said, "'Twas no normal wind pushing at your vessel, but something altogether strange."

I reached up to be sure that my kerchief still covered my hair. Luna's cap and Symon's had been snatched away by the storm.

"Symon!" came a voice from the crowd, and a middle-aged man with a tanned, weathered face and a gap between his front teeth stepped forward. "What on earth happened, lad?"

Symon shook his head, sending sand flying. "A freak wind, Albert," he replied.

"It was no such thing!" Luna objected, but before she could continue, I grabbed her hand and squeezed it hard. Confused, she looked at me, and I gave her the smallest shake of my head.

"We know it was no freak wind," I murmured, low. "I'm sure as can be that it was some magic or enchantment. But we mustn't draw more attention to ourselves." Luna's eyes lit with excitement, and she squeezed my hand back, signaling that she understood.

Albert whistled and walked around the *Cateline*, its bow half-buried in the sand. "I've never seen the like," he said. "Your boat will need some work, that's certain."

"Aye, that it will," Symon said ruefully, looking at the mastless, battered craft.

"That's nothing you cannot fix," said the red-cheeked woman. "You, Albert, take Jean and bring down the spruce trunk from our shed. It's not finished, but Symon can use it for a mast until he can get his own."

"But 'tis ours, Mathilde!" protested Albert.

"Nonsense, Husband," the woman said sternly. "Do

we need two masts? Have we two boats? I think not. Bring the tools as well. You, Symon, go home and get some dry clothes on, and I'll take your guests—" And here she broke off, an inquisitive look on her face. I was ready to leap in with a story, but Luna spoke first.

"We're Symon's cousins," she said, lying with ease. "Distant cousins. We were passing through and stopped to visit. Symon was giving us a taste of the fisherman's life."

"Quite a taste!" Albert said. "I doubt you'll want to feast again at that table!" The others hooted with laughter, and even we, soaked and bruised, had to smile. I could see that Symon was puzzled at Luna's lie, but to my relief he went along with her story.

"Have you dry things at your cousin's cottage?" Madame Mathilde asked us. We shook our heads, and I pointed to our sacks, flung out of the boat onto the sand.

"Those are our spare clothes," I said. It was clear they were as wet as we were.

"Then you will have to borrow," Madame Mathilde ordered. "I've clothes aplenty, for my nine children and five grandchildren come and go and always leave something behind. Follow me."

Trailing like a brood of chicks behind their hen, we went with Madame Mathilde into Vittray. As we trudged up the cobblestoned street, dozens of people on foot walked by in either direction, giving us curious looks. Horse-drawn wagons piled high with goods passed us, carrying items of all sorts from the ships in the harbor to the rest of the kingdom. The noise and bustle were strange and bewildering to me, and I hugged my sodden cloak around me anxiously. Luna was enthralled by the town, though. Several times I had to drag her away from a shop window displaying bolts of cloth or candles of all sizes or breads round, long, and braided. Everything was new to her, after being so long sheltered from the world.

The storm was gone completely, and no breeze blew, yet suddenly I sensed an unnatural chill. A moment later the back of my neck tingled, as though someone were watching me. I looked around, but I saw nothing suspicious among the people we passed in the street. Uneasy, I moved close to Luna and whispered, "I believe that Manon is near."

"Do you really think so?" Luna whispered back, her eyes wide.

"I feel just as I did in the forest yesterday. There's a chill, and a sense of being watched. What else could it be?"

Luna spun about so quickly that I nearly tripped over her. "Where is she?"

"Hush!" I hissed. "I can't see her, but I'm sure that she's close by. Please be careful what you say."

"I wish she would show herself," Luna said in a low voice. "If I could just get my hands on her . . ." I wanted to laugh, imagining Luna against the might of our wicked fairy cousin, but I was also touched. She was like a fierce little banty rooster, my sister, pecking at anything that threatened.

As Symon turned away from us toward his own cottage, Madame Mathilde called, "Lad, come to my house when your repairs are done. I'll have supper for you, and your cousins can bide the night with us. There's room for all."

"I will, Madame Mathilde!" Symon waved and ran down a dirt lane toward a small, neat dwelling.

We soon reached Madame Mathilde's oaken door, which she pushed open to reveal a snug parlor with comfortable chairs and settees. A veritable crowd of people rose and came to greet us. Despite the commotion, I could not keep from yawning hugely. I felt myself drooping, and Madame Mathilde's keen eyes noticed. She did not bother with introductions but simply said, "These are three of my children, and two of their children. Oh, and the baby. We will be more formal when you are dried. Gaby, take these folk upstairs and find them some dry clothes. They've had a bit of a spill, boating."

"I can see that!" the girl, Gaby, said, smiling and hooking her arm through mine. "Come with me, you two, and we'll set you right."

Under the eaves upstairs, we took the bundles of clothes Gaby handed us. I paused as she opened a bedroom door and said, "You can change in here." Should I take Luna into the room with me? After all, she was pretending to be a boy. But we were saved having to choose when Gaby pointed Luna toward another room, and she darted inside.

I stripped off my soaked clothes and brushed the sand from my skin as well as I could. I had just pulled a dry shift over my head when a quick knock sounded and the door opened.

Madame Mathilde stood in the doorway, holding a towel, her lips pursed. "I brought you this, lass," she said. "And I've one for the lad. Or should I say the other lass?"

I blushed and looked at the floor. "Yes, the other lass," I admitted, and she nodded.

"And not just lasses, but princesses both, eh?"

I stared at her, dumbstruck. How did she know?

"I thought as much," she said, shaking her head. "And you should not be surprised to hear that people are looking for you. You and your sister will make things clear to me, I hope."

She left the room as briskly as she'd entered, and I

pulled on the dress Gaby had given me and dried my hair with the towel, braided it, and covered it again with the kerchief. Then I hurried down the stairs to the parlor and sat before the fire, tickling the baby as he lay kicking on the floor while Gaby and the others looked on curiously.

Luna descended, and I could see from her uncomfortable expression that Madame Mathilde had spoken to her too. Madame Mathilde ordered her children and grandchildren to leave us, and they obeyed as meekly as we had when we followed her home.

After the rest of the family was gone, I pulled out the vial of devil's shrub, which luckily had survived the voyage. I gave it to Madame Mathilde, asking if she would make tea, and she quickly did. We sat at the rough table as I sipped and revived. Then the questions began.

"Do you know your father's guards have been searching through the town?" Madame Mathilde demanded. We shook our heads, cowed. "Have you heard that your dear royal mother has taken to her bed, sick with fear and desperation?"

"Oh no!" I cried.

"And that your tutor has been questioned and accused of engineering your disappearance? Soldiers took him from the main square and dragged him away. He may well be in the palace dungeon already."

"Poor Mama," I breathed. "Poor Master Julien! Oh,

Madame Mathilde, can't we send a message to the castle to let them know we're all right?"

"If we do, they'll be here before you can blink," Luna pointed out. "And we'll be back in our rooms, under lock and key. And you'll be asleep!"

I dropped my head into my hands in dismay. Again, Luna was right. It was really quite maddening, how often she'd been right in the last two days.

"Your Highnesses, you must explain yourselves," Madame Mathilde commanded, not at all afraid to tell a princess what to do. She was surely the bossiest woman I had ever met, but I believed she could be trusted.

I raised my head and replied, "Yes, Madame Mathilde, I'll disclose everything. But we must tell our story to Symon as well, for he knows nothing of it. Please let me wait until he comes."

Madame Mathilde frowned, but then she nodded. "In the meantime, we will eat," she said. She brought us more tea—berry tea, this time—and bread and cheese and meat pasties, and we ate ravenously. Before very long, Symon and Albert returned and joined us at the table.

"That's done!" Albert reported cheerfully. "The mast is up, the sail's replaced, and the weakened boards are patched."

"I'm very grateful," Symon said soberly to him and Madame Mathilde. "I will pay you back when I can."

"Don't be foolish, boy," Madame Mathilde chided him. "Bring us ten fat fish and we'll call it even." Symon shook his head, but I could see that he knew better than to argue with her.

"I've told Albert what it is that you seek," Symon informed us. "We can set out again in the morning." He helped himself to the food that Madame Mathilde handed around.

Albert looked doubtful. "I know you've always had the urge in ye to explore, lad," he said, "but those waters is deep, and your boat small. Might be your cousins should find another to take 'em—someone with a hardier vessel."

"And there is something you must know first," I said to Symon, before he could object. "We haven't told you everything. And some of what we have told you isn't entirely true."

I proceeded to explain who we were and what had happened to us, recounting the tale of enchantment old and new, of good fairy and bad. Symon's and Albert's and Madame Mathilde's eyes grew wide with surprise and alarm.

At the story's end, Symon let out a low whistle, much as Albert had done on the strand. "So you're under a curse, and you seek a cure," he said to me, as if trying the idea out.

"Yes," I said softly, and he shook his head in wonder.

Then he turned to Luna. "And you are indeed a girl," he said.

"You knew?" she asked, surprised.

"I guessed—but not that you were a princess." He turned back. "You should have told me." He gave me a look I could not read.

"I don't see why it matters," Luna protested. "Would you have treated us differently if you had known?"

He thought before he answered. "I doubt it," he said at last. "But you should have allowed me to make the choice. My boat was nearly destroyed, and it's my livelihood—though you'd know nothing of that."

His words were harsh, but they were no more than we deserved. "Forgive us," I pleaded. "We were wrong not to tell you. We didn't think we'd be putting you in such danger. I promise, we won't keep secrets from you again."

Symon's furrowed brow smoothed at my apology, and he gave me a tiny, crooked smile. "Very well, Your Highness," he said, and I smiled back, hearing the teasing behind the title.

"A woman selling quill pens," Madame Mathilde mused. "I remember seeing such a woman, this market day past. She was new to the town and wouldn't mingle with the rest of us. It could well have been that Manon. I didn't like the looks of her—and now I know why."

"Have you seen her since?" I asked.

"I have indeed," she said. "She was in the group that gathered round you on the beach. She saw you come into the harbor. I don't doubt that she knows you are with me now."

I thought of the strange feeling I'd had walking up from the harbor and exchanged a horrified glance with Luna. We leaped up and ran to the front window, expecting to see a wizened, foul face staring in at us. The view showed only laden wagons in the street and the townspeople going about their business, but I knew Manon had to be somewhere near.

"We must flee!" I cried, turning back to the others.

Madame Mathilde agreed. "You should go as soon as you can, but I believe that we have something that may help you on your journey." She conferred with Albert, who went to a wooden trunk in the corner of the room and opened it, pulling out a sheaf of parchment. Symon joined him, and they spread the papers out on the floor.

"Maps!" Symon exclaimed, smoothing out one, then another.

"This one, I think," Albert said, pointing. Luna and I peered over Symon's shoulder, trying to make sense of it. The lower right side of the map showed a town, and I realized it was Vittray, its streets and lanes marked and named. To the left was the harbor, and the rest of the map seemed a vast blue emptiness, dotted with a few brown patches.

"Those dots—are they islands?" Symon asked.

"Aye," Albert replied. "Though it's anyone's guess how true the map is. None of us fisherfolk have been out so far. 'Twere my great-uncle Luc who drew it. He were an explorer—as mad as a box of frogs. The sea got to him, I always said."

I imagined sailing through the expanse of blue on the map. All that sameness, all that wind and sun and water, might make a person mad. Then I looked more closely at the islands. They were not just dots. One was shaped like a sickle moon, another had jagged edges that looked sharp and forbidding. A third had a long piece of land that stuck out into the sea like a pointing finger.

Along the top and left-hand side of the map, where it was all ocean, there were drawings of strange, snake-like figures and elegant writing. I crouched over the parchment to see them more clearly and traced the intricate words with my finger. "Does this say, 'Here Be Dragons'?" I asked nervously.

"Mapmakers' language," Albert explained. "It means those parts be unknown."

"So there are really no dragons?"

"Nay," Albert replied with a gap-toothed smile. "I

never heard tell of them in all my years on the sea."

"How can we know which of these islands is Emmeline's?" I asked.

"We cannot," Symon said regretfully. "We'll have to guess. Perhaps we'll be lucky. But even an inaccurate map is better than no map at all."

"You don't need to take us," I assured him. "In fact, you must not. It's too dangerous. But if you could help us find a boat of our own—"

Symon snorted. "And you'll sail yourselves? Begging your pardon, Princess, but you don't know port from starboard. You'd be lost—or worse—in no time."

Luna took offense at his words. "We can surely sail a boat," she insisted. "If you can do it, I'm certain that most anyone can. We don't need you to help us."

"Luna!" I scolded.

"It's the job of a lifetime, to learn to sail on these waters." Madame Mathilde's tone was not at all kind.

"And of course I'll take you, Princess," Symon said to me, ignoring Luna completely. "We've made a bargain, and I'll stick to it."

I was greatly relieved, and thanked him sincerely. "But you must not address me as 'Princess' or 'Your Highness,'" I said. "We're friends, just as when you thought we were common travelers."

Symon grinned. "All right then, Deckhand," he said. "But it's clear that we must go at once."

"Are we to sail at night then?" Luna asked eagerly. I shivered with fear and anticipation, thinking of how dark the waters would be, how cold the wind.

"Do we have a choice?" Symon replied. "Otherwise, we'd just be waiting for your cousin Manon to find us, like beasts ready for slaughter. I don't think I'd get much sleep under those circumstances."

So it was decided. We gathered our things together. Madame Mathilde gave us food and clean clothes, and Albert and Symon pored over the map and chose one island of the three to aim for. They picked the sickle-shaped one, as it was closest and might have a safe harbor at its protected center. Then Symon rolled up the parchment and stowed it with the food. Albert bowed to us, and Madame Mathilde tried to curtsy, but I raised her up and took her hands.

"We'll be back soon," I said fiercely, "and then my father will reward you for your kind assistance."

"Only come back safe and wide awake," Madame Mathilde replied, enfolding me in her strong arms. In her embrace, breathing in her warm cinnamon scent, I felt more secure than I had since I had pricked my finger. How I wished I could rest there for a while!

"When we're safely away, will you get word to our parents that we are well?" I asked her. "I can't bear thinking that Mama suffers over us—or that Master Julien might be punished for our disappearance."

"As soon as you go," she vowed. Then she released me with a final pat. "Now, let's be sure that no one watches you as you leave."

The house had a back door, and we crept out of it into a narrow alleyway, checking first to be certain no one lurked there. Albert led us through twisting lanes down to the harbor, where the repaired *Cateline* rested at the water's edge, its mast once more rising high.

We clambered into the boat and took seats, and Albert pushed it off the sand into the water. "Good luck to ye," he said gruffly. "Sail straight, lad!"

"I will, Albert," Symon promised. He pulled the ropes to raise the sail and the wind caught it, pushing us westward, toward the sinking sun. Then he gave the lines to me and clambered back into the stern to tend the tiller. As we eased our way out of the harbor, I looked back at Vittray. Shading my eyes with my hand, I gazed at the red-tiled roofs, at the anchored boats and the long pier, wondering when I would see the town again. And then I gasped in shock.

At the very end of the pier stood a woman, dressed all in black, cloaked and hooded. As I watched, the wind snatched her hood and pulled it back. I saw a wrinkled face, a deep scowl, and piercing eyes that seemed to bore into my own. It was Manon.

10

Of a Legend
Come to Life

I felt her gaze on me as the wind whipped her long gray hair back from her face. I had known she was near, but to see her cruel expression was a terrible shock. Her dark eyes stared into mine with a hatred that chilled me far more than my fear of the shadowy water before and below us. Why should she loathe me so? Was it all because of a love thwarted more than a century ago?

I fully expected Manon to raise another storm, to push us back onto the beach with gale winds, but she did not. She simply watched as we sailed away from the lights of town and into the dimming evening. I shivered, and Symon reached forward and patted my hand, his touch warm and comforting. Of course Luna, who saw everything, turned and noticed this, but she managed to refrain from making a rude comment.

"I suppose," Symon said, "that was Manon?"

Luna called back, "It must have been. I don't know what she has in mind for us."

"Well," Symon said, "she knows we're going. So I expect she will do something to try to stop us."

"Perhaps she just believes we will drown ourselves, and she won't have to lift a finger." The wind swallowed my words, yet Symon heard them. He gave me a sympathetic smile. I tried to smile back, but I could not. I was bruised from our wild ride onto the sand, and frightened by the great expanse of ocean before us. I was worried about my mother. And I was so terribly tired. The tea could control my desire to slumber for a time, but always it crept back. I longed to curl up on the hard wooden bench of the *Cateline* and close my eyes. At that moment, I wished that I could sleep for a hundred years.

A wave of drowsiness came over me. *No, no!* I thought in desperation. *I didn't mean it! I want to stay awake!* I grabbed for Luna. When she felt my touch she looked back, and at the sight of my panicked expression, she spun around.

"I cannot stay awake!" I cried.

"But you just had tea," Luna reminded me.

"It doesn't matter! I thought . . . oh, it was so stupid! I wished to fall asleep, and suddenly the urge was so much stronger. Oh, help me, please!"

In one quick move, Luna leaned over the side, scooped up a palmful of water, and flung it into my face. "There you are," she said obligingly.

I gasped and sputtered and blinked the salt from my eyes. For a moment I was angry, but I was wide awake again.

"Thank you," I said grudgingly, and Luna laughed and replied, "Any time, Sister!"

We sailed on as the sun gave up its light, and no unnatural storm came to push us back to land. On Symon's command, Luna climbed back to join him in the stern, and he handed her a strange little box that he called a compass. Then he instructed her on how to use it.

"You see," he said, "this needle always points to the north." I leaned toward them and watched as he turned the compass box. Indeed, there was a needle inside, mounted on a pin, and as the box turned the needle swiveled as well, always pointing in the same direction. Symon went on, "We're going to turn due north, so you want to be sure we are aimed this way." He showed Luna a little mark on the compass box.

"How does it work?" I asked, intrigued. "Is it magic?"

Symon laughed. "The magic of science," he said. "The compass needle is attracted to the magnetism of the earth, which is strongest in the north." I puzzled over this as Luna twirled the compass, pleased with the constancy of the needle pointing north.

"Let me know if we veer off course," Symon told Luna. "We should see the island before morning—that is, if we don't miss it completely."

"Oh, we won't miss it," Luna assured him. "This map reading isn't so hard. We're right on course, I'm pretty certain." I rolled my eyes. I wouldn't have put Luna in charge of navigation, but I did have faith in Symon and his skill with tiller and sail.

When the moon rose, three-quarters full, it cast a silver trail on the water that lighted our way like a beacon. To pass the time, Symon taught us the words to the poem he'd recited to us the day before, and the tune that the fisherman of Vittray had set it to:

Like an eagle caged, I pine,
On this dull, unchanging shore:
Oh! give me the flashing brine,
The spray and the tempest's roar!

A life on the ocean wave,
A home on the rolling deep,

Where the scattered waters rave,
And the winds their revels keep!

We sang as loudly as we could, and all at once, I saw pale shapes leaping through the gentle swells. Drawn by our voices, dolphins arced through the air, one after another. Luna cried out in delight as they came almost close enough to touch. I reached out my hand, and one swam right to me and raised its long nose to my palm. I stroked its warm, smooth skin, and its bright eye winked at me before it dove deep again.

"So beautiful!" I said to Symon.

"Aye, they always look to me as if they're smiling," he replied.

The water was clear enough and the moonlight bright enough that I could see them as they plunged, and it seemed to me that another figure swam with them for a time, not dolphin but not quite human, either. It reminded me of the shape we'd seen in the air when we'd first met Symon. I recalled what he'd said about lutins: *They can fly through the air without wings and swim through the water without gills.* The figure wove among the sleek white dolphins in a graceful sea dance. I was about to call the others' attention to it, but suddenly the swimmers all veered off and were gone, and I decided to keep it to myself.

After that the hours seemed to blend together. The only sign of time passing was the changing position of the stars as they wheeled through the heavens, and the sinking of the moon. We were silent, and I began once more my struggle with Sleep as the boat sped rhythmically over the waves. I pinched my arms, counted stars, and bit my lips so hard it hurt. I splashed cold water on my cheeks, but it didn't rouse me as when Luna had done it.

Suddenly Luna called out, "Land ho!"

I peered through the ocean darkness and made out a shape that was darker still. "Is it truly land?" I asked.

"Aye, it is!" Symon replied. He used the tiller to aim the *Cateline* toward the low-lying mass. I ducked as the boom swung around.

Symon's plan was to approach the island between the points of the sickle's curve, where there might be a natural bay. "We should wait for daylight," I advised nervously. If there were treacherous rocks, they would be hidden by the night.

"I have no anchor line long enough to hold us here," Symon replied. "This water is far deeper than the places where I fish, and I didn't think to bring extra rope. We'll have to try to land."

He set Luna to watch off the port side and me off the starboard side, ready to call out if we saw rocks or any other danger. But there was nothing to fear. Tacking against the wind now, we zigzagged between the crescent's arms and sailed into the protected bay, sliding to a halt on sand so pearl white that it glowed in the starlight.

We clambered out of the *Cateline* and struggled to pull it up onto the beach so it would not wash back out to sea. We could see little beyond the strand; dunes rose up, and behind them a line of trees faded into darkness.

"I'll build a fire," Symon said. I heard no sound at all besides the noise we made searching for dried driftwood, no call of owl or night animal. Even the wind had died completely. The silence seemed eerie, but I said nothing, not wanting to share my uneasiness with the others.

We built a small pile of driftwood, and Symon struck a spark with flint. In a moment a fire blazed and crackled with a comforting noise. I made my tea while the others drank the fresh water we carried, and we ate and warmed our chilled hands gratefully.

"I slept a bit on the boat," Luna told Symon. "You rest now; I'll stay awake with Aurora."

Symon curled up beside the fire and was asleep in minutes. How I envied him! I sat beside Luna as close to the flames as I dared. I didn't want to think about what could be lurking beyond the small light cast by the fire.

Try as she might to stay alert, Luna too dozed off before long. I didn't wake her, for I didn't feel the usual pull of Sleep. Something about this lonely place made me anxious and drove away the tiredness. I was learning to trust my feelings. I would not relax my vigil.

As the fire died and the horizon began, ever so slightly, to lighten, I heard a scratching sound. I swiveled from left to right, peering into the dark to see what approached. The noise came closer, and my heart began to beat faster. Then, at the top of one of the dunes, a dark shape appeared, and then another, and another. As the sun slowly rose, I could finally make out their forms, and I recoiled in horror. Four-legged and taller than dogs, their eyes glowed orange, and they stared straight at me.

"Wake up!" I screamed, shocking the others out of their sleep. "There are wolves on the dunes!"

Symon was up in an instant, Luna close behind him. Symon pulled a short knife from his boot and swung it wildly about in a circle, but the animals kept their distance. As the light strengthened, I could see them more clearly, and I began to tremble in earnest.

They were not wolves after all, as frightening as that would have been. I had never seen, nor even imagined, creatures such as these. They were as big as donkeys or small horses, though most of their size was muscled body atop short, stubby legs. Their fur, like their eyes, was reddish-orange. Their heads resembled boars' heads, with tiny piglike ears and long curved tusks, but their mouths gaped open and were crowded with sharp, crooked teeth. Their tails, long and thick and tipped with white, swung slowly from side to side.

"Oh, what are they?" Luna whispered shakily.

"We must flee, or we'll be torn limb from limb," Symon said in a low voice. "They are the Beasts of Gevadan."

Of Beasts
and Bravery

The look on Symon's face alarmed me almost as much as the creatures themselves. "What are the Beasts of Gevadan?" I gasped.

"Later!" Symon urged. "Come, slowly. Quietly." He took my hand and Luna's, and we began backing toward the boat. As we inched along, the beasts pressed forward. My heart was beating so hard that I could feel it quiver inside my chest.

"Will they eat us?" I whispered.

"The stories say—," Symon began, but then he

stopped. I was glad. I didn't really want to know the answer.

As we tried to move toward the place where the *Cateline* rested on the sand, the beasts advanced craftily with their snouts to the ground. Before we knew it, they had circled around and were between us and the boat. We had no choice but to retreat slowly inland over the beach grass, herded by the creatures as if they were sheepdogs and we their flock. We stumbled backward, up over the dunes, into a stretch of scrub that ended at a forest's edge.

"If we reach the woods, we could climb a tree," I said, low. "Surely with those legs, they can't climb."

"We would be treed prey then," Symon replied. "I think that's what they want. They could wait until we weakened and starved and dropped like ripe fruit."

"Have you no weapon? You ought to have a weapon!" Luna said, and Symon shook his head.

"Only my fishing knife. It's too short, and they are too many." He paused, then said, "Do you see that stretch of sand along the edge of the forest? The woods meet the sea just past it. If we can get to the water there, we can wade out to where it would be over their heads. Then we can try to get back to the boat before they figure out what we're doing."

I could see that there was a sweep of bright, clean

sand off to our right, and that, as Symon had said, it met the trees as they curved around to the water's edge. Luna was a very fast runner, I knew. She always bested me in footraces and could escape from me when I tried to catch and punish her for her wrongdoings. I had no doubt that Symon was quick too. If the beasts were slowed by their stubby legs, perhaps the two of them could reach the water in time. But I was not speedy. And I was further hampered by my long skirts. Suddenly I envied Luna her boys' clothing. We had no choice, though, and I readied myself as Symon said, "On my count, then. One . . . two . . . three!"

Together, we spun and sprinted with all our might. Surprised, the beasts stood stupidly for a moment, and then they sprang after us. As I'd suspected, though, they were not fast, and their pig noses made breathing difficult. We could hear them rasping and snorting behind us. In a moment Luna was ahead of me, and she reached the stretch of sand quickly, even before Symon.

But within a stride or two, it was clear that this was not ordinary sand. Her boots sank in to their tops and then over, and she seemed unable to pull her legs out. She thrashed wildly, and in a moment, she was up to her thighs in the sand.

"Quicksand!" Symon shouted. "Aurora, leap onto it. Land on your knees, and spread yourself so you lie flat!"

Without thinking, I jumped when he did, and we landed with a splat on hands and knees and quickly lay down, our arms and legs outstretched to spread our weight more evenly. My face was pressed against the wet sand, which surged under me almost as if it were water.

"Don't struggle," Symon called to Luna. "Don't try to pull your feet out, or you'll be sucked under."

I raised my head and saw that Luna had stopped moving, and that stopped her descent. The beasts did not fare as well. They plunged into the sand after us and at once began to sink, yelping and writhing in their brutish panic as the sand drew them lower and lower. One of them had leaped almost close enough to me to touch, and I gazed into its dreadful piggy eyes as they rolled back in terror. It flung itself back and forth in desperation as first its stubby limbs, then its thick torso, and finally its vile toothy face were covered by the sucking sands. Three of the beasts died like this, with the others left pacing at the edge of the quick-sand, their white-tipped tails flicking back and forth. When their companions had disappeared entirely, they opened their mouths and howled, an eerie, horrid sound that made goose bumps rise on my skin. Then they turned and lumbered back into the forest, leaving us to our fates.

"Luna," I cried, "are you all right?"

"I'm still alive," she called back, "but this monstrous sand won't let me go!"

"Stay still," Symon ordered. "Aurora, you and I must swim to the other side and find a long branch. Then we can use it to pull Luna out."

"Swim?" I protested. "But it's sand!"

"Sand and water, both," Symon replied. "If you keep your weight evenly atop it, it can't pull you down. Wriggle as if you were paddling in the sea."

I had never paddled in the sea in my life, but I began to squirm across the sand. To my astonishment, it worked. Symon and I moved like snakes with wretched slowness to the far side of the lake of quicksand.

When I turned my head to check on Luna, I realized that she was sinking again, ever so slowly, though she was as still as a statue. The sand was now up to her hips, and her face was twisted with fear. "We must hurry!" I cried. "The sand is dragging her down!"

Symon got to solid land and scrambled out, hauling me the last few feet. He ran for the trees, searching for a branch that we could use to reach Luna.

Unwilling to let my sister out of my sight, I stood in agony on the shore. Luna held her hands above her head as she sank steadily to her waist. Her frantic eyes met mine across the sand.

"What if it should cover my nose?" she gasped.

"Hurry!" I shrieked.

Symon sprinted from the forest's edge, carrying a long, sturdy branch. He stopped at the verge of the quicksand and said to me, "Slide back onto the sand."

I took a deep breath and flung myself full length on the shifting lake of sand and water. Symon passed me the branch, and I held it out to Luna.

She could not reach it.

She stretched her arms out as far as she could, but the end of the branch was inches away from her clutching fingers. Her efforts caused the sand to grasp at her, and she sank still further.

Symon quickly saw the problem. He spread himself on the quicksand, with just his feet on the shore to anchor him, and took hold of my ankles. I moved forward. Then, as the sand covered Luna's shoulders and crept up her neck, she reached again for the branch. Her fingers closed on wood.

Symon wriggled backward, dragging me as I held the branch that Luna also gripped. When he got to solid ground, he began pulling in earnest. I thought my arms would leave their sockets. I was sure that I could not keep hold of the branch, but somehow I did.

Slowly, slowly, up Luna rose as the sands tried their best to keep her: Shoulders emerged, then waist, legs, then at last, with a gurgle, her bare feet. The hungry sand had eaten her boots.

It was quick work after that. We slithered to the far side of the quicksand, and in a moment I found myself sprawled on the hard ground with Luna in my arms. We were both sobbing, covered from head to toe in wet, sticky sand.

"I'm sorry," I said again and again, hugging my sister as tightly as I could. "Oh, Luna, I'm so sorry!"

"But you saved me, Aurora!" she protested, her face smeared with tears and muck.

"It was my fault you were in danger at all. It's my job to keep you safe!"

"We can't stay," Symon urged. "The beasts may return."

Unsteadily, Luna and I rose to our feet. Symon put his arm around me, helping me to stay upright.

"I believe I've grown a few inches," I remarked shakily.

Symon managed a grin, his teeth white against his filthy face, and Luna said, "I'll miss my boots. I'd just broken them in!"

I laughed weakly. Then we stumbled the few yards to the shore, testing every step on sand to be sure it held us and glancing back often to check for the beasts. At the water we tried to wash off the sand, but it clung. Finally I just sat in the sea and let the little waves lap over me. My clothes were heavy with grit, and my hair was thick with it. There was even sand in my eyebrows. I dunked my head and rinsed and rinsed, and the others did the same. At last we stood, dripping but clean, and waded back toward the strand where the *Cateline* rested, Symon and I carrying our shoes.

The sun was warm and began to dry us as we walked along the curved shoreline, and I felt my strength returning. "Tell me, Captain," I said, "what are the Beasts of Gevadan?"

"Well, I didn't think there was any proof that they still existed—or rather, there was no proof before today," Symon said. "But long ago, creatures that were thought to be part wolf and part wild boar attacked the town of Gevadan, a hundred leagues or more to the south of Vittray. I'd heard they killed dozens of people. It's a tale told round the fire on a winter's eve now."

"Killed them how?" I asked in a small voice.

"Some say the victims were torn to bits. Other reports have the beasts sucking out their preys' blood and livers." I shivered, and even Luna faltered a little. I changed the subject quickly.

"And how did you know that was quicksand?" I asked Symon.

"I've seen it before," he replied. "The marshes to the north are full of it."

"Quicksand, the Beasts of Gevadan—we hardly need a tutor with you here!" Luna teased him.

Symon smiled, but I suddenly thought of Master Julien, perhaps locked in the castle dungeon. I hoped that Madame Mathilde had sent word to Papa and Mama that he was not to blame for our disappearance.

We reached the boat and the cold campfire and found our belongings undisturbed. "The beasts didn't even take our food," Luna said, pleased.

"That doesn't mean they won't be back," Symon pointed out. "Let's go, quickly." We picked up our things, piled everything into the batteau, and pushed it into the water. When we were all on board, I drew a deep breath and looked back at the island. It looked peaceful enough—sun and dappled sand and forest.

"The Island of Beasts," I said with a shudder.

"Luna, mark it on the map," Symon instructed. "Now you are a cartographer, and this is your first discovery."

Luna started to laugh, a little hysterically. "A cartographer—what's that?" she gasped. "Someone who builds carts?"

Symon raised an eyebrow. "A cartographer is a map-maker."

"You should know that, Luna," I added. "It's from the Latin *carta*, meaning . . ." I paused, waiting for her to finish.

But by then Luna was laughing too hard to give the definition, even if she had known it, and I started to laugh too. Symon joined in as much with relief as amusement, and still laughing, he raised the sail as we glided over the waves away from the Island of Beasts.

12

Of a Siren and Her Song

The *Cateline* seemed a haven of safety after the Island of Beasts. When our wild laughter had died away, we sat awhile in silence, regaining our strength. Soon, though, I began to yawn, feeling the familiar pull of Sleep. I leaned over the side to splash water on my face, and was stopped by my own reflection. I looked nothing at all like a princess—exhausted and pale, my hair tangled, my kerchief lost to the quicksand.

Then I glimpsed again a shape swimming below us. Had the dolphins returned? The reflection of the sun on the water made it hard to see into the depths.

The figure twisted beneath us. I squinted, and for an instant I saw the lutin clearly.

He did not move like a man. His legs swung up and down like a dolphin's tail, speeding him along as quickly as we sailed. He turned his head upward. His face was beautiful, like a statue's, and his eyes, the exact greenish-blue color of the sea, met mine as I stared from above. He winked, and I gasped, pulling back quickly.

"What is it?" Symon asked. "Are there sharks?"

I leaned over and looked down again. The lutin was gone. Why was he following us? Was he in Manon's employ?

"I thought . . . no, never mind." I didn't want to scare the others. "It was just a trick of the light. But I am getting so tired—is there any way to make tea?"

Luna sprang into action, as much as she could spring in the confines of the little boat. She dug out a flask of fresh water from our bags, and I handed her the vial of devil's shrub. "We can let the sun steep it," she said, sprinkling some of the precious herb into the flask. "But there's not much of the powder left. Drink as little as you dare, Sister!"

I waited for the tea to brew, resisting the temptation to look once more into the water to see if the lutin was still there. In the warm sunshine, our clothes soon dried, stiff with salt from our bath in the ocean. The scratchiness helped to keep me awake. At last Luna proclaimed the tea ready, and I took a gulp of the bitter elixir, grateful to feel a rush of wakefulness and energy.

"Luna!" Symon called from the stern. "Get out the map and compass and set us on our course. We'll try for the next island."

Luna pulled out the parchment map and looked down at it, a frown on her face. "That one looks dangerous," she said. "See, the map shows that the coast is all rocky."

"We'll get close, and if it seems too risky, we'll turn away," Symon instructed. "But if your aunt doesn't want to be found, it stands to reason that she would hide somewhere dangerous or difficult. If I had an enemy like Manon, I would hide in the most inaccessible place I could find."

"You *have* an enemy like Manon—Manon herself," I pointed out. "She's no friend to you now that you're helping us."

"Aye, but she will never catch the *Cateline*!" Symon vowed, and I tugged the sail tight so it seized the wind and sent us speeding over the water.

We were becalmed for a time in the early afternoon, and it was terrible. The wind simply died, and we couldn't move at all. The sun beat down, making us very hot and thirsty. I worried that I would become burned and pulled the hood of my servant's cloak up for a time, trying to protect my face, but it was just too hot. Luna, of course, did not care; she even rolled up her sleeves, and her arms browned in the sun.

"Do you think this is Manon's doing?" I asked Symon. He shook his head.

"It feels natural to me," he said. "I know that she can raise a great wind, but I don't think she can cause the wind to die. It's a very different thing."

"What do sailors do when they're becalmed?" Luna asked, clearly bored.

"Oh, anything they can think of. Sing, drink, mend the sails and the nets . . . talk."

"Well," Luna said, coming back to sit next to me on my bench, "we've sung already, and we're low on water for drinking. Nothing needs mending. I'm for talking."

"When aren't you?" I teased.

She made a face at me. "So, Symon, tell us: Isn't it lonely living by yourself in your cottage? And in a cave on the shore?"

"Luna!" I was dismayed at her intrusive question.

But Symon didn't mind. "I'm used to it now," he replied. "At first, though, after my mother died, it was terrible. My friends were busy with their own lives. I'd no one to speak to at all. I talked to myself a lot. People thought I was a bit mad for a while. Then Madame Mathilde and Albert came to me and said I had to dine at their house of a Sunday, and that was enough to settle me. I just needed some people to be with."

"Oh," I said softly. I could hardly imagine such loneliness.

"How awful!" Luna said. "Sometimes I've wanted to be by myself, because we're always watched, but that's different. I don't know what I'd do without Aurora to talk to."

I was startled. Luna and I more often argued than talked. But when I thought about it, I knew what she meant. We shared our lives. We knew each other, even if we didn't always get along.

"And you, Deckhand," Symon said to me, "do you long for silence and solitude?"

"I love to be alone," I admitted. "But it's as Luna said—I think I only like it because I have others to be with if I choose. Sometimes, though . . ." I trailed off.

"What?" Symon prompted.

"Sometimes I think about when I'll be queen. I won't be alone ever then. I'll be surrounded by courtiers, and I'll always have people needing and wanting things from me. I fear it will be unbearable." I didn't mention the nightmares I'd had, where people I didn't know followed me and grabbed at me, their faces desperate, pleading for help I couldn't give them.

"I think you'll be good at it," Luna said, surprising me again. "You're smart, and you're kind. Papa is both those things, and he's a good king, isn't he?"

"When you're queen, if you should need a respite, you can come out with me on my boat," Symon said. "I'll have a special cushioned, embroidered throne-bench installed just for you. We'll sail away from your subjects for an hour or two."

Luna hooted at this, but though I knew he was joking, I found the idea comforting. And then a small breeze fluttered into the sail and puffed it back into life. We cheered as once again we began to move. "West-northwest," Luna proclaimed, back on her bench and working the compass with great concentration and self-importance.

As the sun sank lower in the sky, we sighted the second island. Its steep cliffs rose up from the sea, and there were enormous rocks jutting out of the water all around it. The island looked as barren and desolate as it had on the map, and I could see no way to get close to shore that would not be perilous.

"We'll circle it," Symon decided, "and see if there is a safer approach."

From every angle, though, the island looked the same, ringed by a jumble of boulders that threatened certain disaster to the *Cateline* if we should draw near. Foamy breakers crashed against the tall cliffs.

"We'll have to turn away," Symon said regretfully. "There's no strand, and no safe channel."

"Wait," said Luna. "What's that?" She pointed at one of the tall gray rocks nearest the shore. Little waves lapped around it, and a figure perched on top. At first we thought it must be a bird; then, as we drew closer, we thought it a seal, but soon we could see that it was a woman, alone atop the stone, her long fair hair waving in the sea breeze.

"How on earth did she get up there? Oh, maybe she's been shipwrecked!" Luna exclaimed. "We should rescue her!"

"Could it be Emmeline?" I grew excited. If this was her island, perhaps she waited there to welcome us!

"Listen," Symon said, an urgency in his tone. The woman had begun to sing.

Though we were far away still, we could hear the singer as if she were right beside us. Her song was wordless, achingly beautiful. In tones as high and pure as the call of a lark or a celestial harp, she sang of desire and heartache, of love found and lost. I reached up and found my face wet with tears, though I did not know why I wept. We sailed closer to her as she sang, and now I could make out her willowy form, her full red lips. And I was shocked to see, curving around the column of rock, her long, silvery, scaled fish's tail.

"Turn about!" Luna shouted suddenly. The *Cateline* had kept to its course, and I realized what Luna was

warning against—we were fast approaching the boulders along the island's coastline. The wind pushed us
swiftly, and in a moment Symon was steering us among
the enormous rocks. The boat twisted and turned, just
missing one and then the next, and I flinched as we
brushed by stone after giant stone.

"We must go back!" I begged Symon in distress. I saw
that his eyes were glazed, his mouth slack. "Turn the
boat!" I shouted. "We'll hit the rocks and sink!" But
Symon didn't seem to hear me.

Luna spun in her seat. "It's the song!" she said.
"Somehow it's enchanted him." She shouted at him,
"Idiot! Plug up your ears!" But Symon would not stop
his ears. He was utterly mesmerized.

I tried to catch Symon's eye, to bring him back to
himself. His rapt attention to the mermaid disturbed
me more than I would have expected. "Rouse yourself!"
I urged him, reaching back to pull on his sleeve, then
slapping his hand. He didn't respond at all.

We were heading straight for the jagged pillar where
the mermaid perched. If we hit it, the *Cateline* would
shatter into bits, and we all would be thrown into the
water and drowned in the crashing waves.

And then I had a sudden thought. Over the relentless song, I called out to Luna, "Do you recall when we
read the story of Odysseus?"

"No," she replied, her eyes on the mermaid.

"Oh, you must!" I cried in frustration. "He was returning home from the battle of Troy with his men. Don't you remember when Odysseus's ship approached the Sirens—the mermaid women who sang men to their deaths?"

Luna turned. "Wait, I do remember!" she said, excited. "The men had to plug up their ears with wax so they couldn't hear the song. We shall do the same! Do we have any wax?"

We hadn't brought candles. I despaired.

Luna stood up, rocking the boat. "The new mast! If it's a pine trunk, there may still be some pine pitch on it—sticky pine pitch. As good as wax!" I recalled the tutor who had mysteriously found pine pitch in his hair, and realized that Luna knew this from experience. Again her troublemaking served a useful end.

Luna scrambled over her seat to the mast, and I ran my hands down it. It was rough, and sticky as well, the pitch oozing from places where small branches had been hurriedly cut in the rush to repair the boat.

"Yes!" I crowed. "Here, you roll it into balls, and I'll stop his ears." Quickly Luna scraped the black, tarry stuff off the mast and rolled it into little spheres. She passed them to me, and I climbed to the stern, where Symon sat hypnotized. He batted me away halfheartedly as I tried to place the pitch in his ears, but his attention was fixed on the mermaid. At last I managed it, pushing the pitch in firmly.

As soon as he could no longer hear the Siren, Symon blinked in sudden awareness of the rocks that now threatened on all sides.

"Hold the tiller!" he shouted to me.

He leaped to grab the ropes and lower the sail before the wind drove us into the boulders. I grasped the tiller, straining to hold it straight. I hadn't realized how much strength it took to keep us on course. When the sail fell, we slowed to a near stop.

We were very close to the mermaid now, seated high on her pillar. Her glorious golden hair made mine look like straw, and her green eyes were luminous. How beautiful she was! She flapped her scaly tail against the side of the rock and furrowed her perfect brow. She seemed vexed that we had stopped our approach, and her song grew louder and more intense.

Just beyond her rock, something stuck up from the water, and I gasped when I realized it was the top of a mast. Another boat had been drawn here by the mermaid's song, and sunk. I turned away, shuddering to think of the sailors who had perished, lying in their watery graves beneath us.

"Are you all right now?" I asked Symon.

"What?" he shouted, deafened by the pitch.

"Are you all right?" I shouted.

"Are you talking to me?" Symon bellowed back.

"Stop yelling!" Luna roared, though she knew Symon would not be able to hear her. I felt the same hysterical laughter rising that had overcome us earlier, but the looming rocks and the mast from the wrecked ship quickly made me serious again. Symon held out oars, and Luna and I used ours to push away from the nearest boulders. Symon began to row as hard as he could to move us back out to sea. Behind us, the bewitching voice faded gradually, until I could no longer hear it at all.

When we were safely out of sight of the mermaid, we stopped so Symon could remove the pine pitch from his ears. It clung to his skin and hair and left black streaks on his cheeks. Luna and I had it on our hands as well.

Symon raised the sail again, and it caught the wind as I bent over the side to try to rinse my hands of the sticky stuff. The cold seawater only caused it to harden. "Oh, what a mess!" I fumed, giving up at last. I would just have to live with the dirt, as I did with the sand and salt that wouldn't wash off.

When Symon came back to take the tiller, I climbed from the stern of the boat back to my place beside the mast. He looked rather shamefaced and was quiet as we sailed. I recalled the expression on his face as the mermaid sang, and despite the danger we had just escaped, I couldn't help smiling. It was clear that Luna was amused as well.

"Well, Luna," I said, "what should we name this island?"

She turned on her bench to face me. "Hmmm. Should it be Mermaid Island? Or perhaps Isle of the Easily Fooled?"

"That's hardly fair!" Symon protested. "It wasn't my fault—it was an enchantment of some sort."

"An enchantment that works only on boys?" Luna scoffed. "Aurora and I weren't bothered in the least."

"I think that was the mermaid Melusine." Symon's voice was somber. "She's said to sing sailors to their deaths. I didn't know that she only enchanted men. There are rarely women on ships, so no one ever talks about what happens when women hear her. But it seems that her song didn't affect you."

Luna laughed. "Or we are simply stronger than you are!"

"Oh, Luna," I chided, seeing how mortified Symon was, "we shouldn't torment him anymore."

"I suppose not," she allowed. "But in future, Captain, when Melusine calls, don't be so quickly charmed!"

I smiled at Symon, who flushed with embarrassment.

"Yes, he was easily charmed," I teased. "But I think he couldn't help it. She was very beautiful."

Symon reached over the side of the boat and tried to splash me in revenge, but only succeeded in wetting my skirt. I laughed and splashed him back. We had been so often wet in recent days that it made no difference anymore.

"We'll call it Melusine's Isle," Luna decided. "I'll mark it on the map, and sailors will know to steer clear if they value their lives." She pulled out the map and noted the island's name.

"Chart our course to the next island, Mate," Symon instructed her. "That's the last of them—let's hope it's your godmother Emmeline's. The sun is getting low, and we should try to find a place to land while it's still light."

It would be dinnertime at Castle Armelle, but I knew that Mama would not be able to eat with us gone. I imagined Papa bringing a tray to her bedside, with tea and the rose-water pudding she loved. Perhaps she could manage a little pudding. Perhaps she would not grow weaker as we moved farther across the sea. Oh, if only we could find Emmeline!

Luna shook her head doubtfully, gazing down at the map. "It looks far," she told Symon. "Farther than from Vittray to the Island of Beasts. And if we miss it—well, beyond that, there's just ocean."

"Then we must be sure not to miss it," Symon said sensibly. "We'll have to sail at night again and use the compass to keep us on course."

I was still thrumming with nerves from our encounter with Melusine, but I felt the beginnings of the familiar pull of Sleep. Moving carefully—I was much better now at getting about without rocking the little craft—I rummaged through our stores and found the remainder of the tea that Luna had made earlier. Then I distributed more water, bread, cheese, and meat from our dwindling supplies.

We ate and sailed on for an hour or so, as the sunset streaked the sky with red and gold. I scanned the horizon for a sign of the next island, but all was just endless water and sky. Not even dolphins disturbed the glassy sea.

Then Symon said, in a rather strange voice, "What's that?" He pointed west. At first I could see nothing. The setting sun nearly blinded me. When my eyes adjusted, I could make out a dark, batlike form far in the distance.

"Is it a bird?" I wondered aloud. "An enormous albatross, perhaps?"

"Albatrosses are mostly white," Symon informed me. "I don't think it's a bird. I think it's a sail."

"A sail!" I exclaimed. "Have you a spyglass, Symon?"

"I don't," Symon replied regretfully. "And I can't make out a flag or a design from this distance."

"Luna will be able to see it," I said.

"Can you tell if it's marked in any way?" Symon asked her.

Luna squinted into the glare of the sun for a long moment, and then shook her head slowly.

"The sail is plain and black. There are no markings, nor any flag."

Symon whistled. "Even pirates fly their flags to frighten their victims. I can think of no one who would sail an unmarked boat."

"No one except—" I stopped, filled with dread.

Luna finished for me. "No one except Manon."

"Quickly!" Symon ordered. "We must move fast enough to lose her!"

"To the north!" Luna called to Symon, holding up the compass to be sure of our bearings. "If we can get to the third island and sail around it quickly, we may be able to find a place to hide the boat and ourselves."

Symon swung the tiller, and the *Cateline* jerked hard to the right. We wobbled on our benches, and I saw Luna lose her balance and reach out to steady herself. And a moment later, with no warning at all, she stood and, to my horror, leaped over the side of the boat into the water.

Of a Damsel's Dire Deed

I couldn't believe it. I couldn't understand it. It looked as if she had jumped, but that made no sense. Had she fallen somehow? Had something dragged her into the water? My voice high with panic, I shouted, "Man overboard!"

Symon sprang up, rocking the boat, and scrambled up to Luna's seat. He peered over the side. "I can't see her!" he called. "I'm going after her! Aurora, hold the tiller."

"She can't swim!" I wailed.

"But she told me . . . ," Symon said, and I shook my head.

"She can't swim," I repeated as I began to weep.

Symon pulled off his boots and plunged into the sea. It was clear that he could swim, and well. He dove downward and was out of sight in a minute. I wiped my eyes on my sleeve and loosened the ropes that held the sail so it lay slack. Then I climbed back to the stern and held the tiller tight. I could see Manon's boat approaching quickly from the west, and I began to tremble.

It seemed to take forever for Symon to reappear, but finally he came to the surface, holding Luna by the collar of her tunic. And with him, an arm around Luna's waist, was the swimmer I had seen with the dolphins and again after we'd left the Island of Beasts—the lutin with the turquoise eyes.

Luna kicked and coughed as Symon and the lutin pushed her into the *Cateline*. Then the lutin boosted Symon in and hung off the side of the boat.

Symon took the tiller from me, and I scrambled forward to where Luna huddled. "Luna, are you all right? Whatever happened? What were you thinking?" I asked frantically, but for once she was silent.

"How do you do?" the lutin said suddenly, and I turned to stare at him.

Even in my panicked state, I had to admit that he was very, very handsome. His perfect features made Symon's tar-streaked face and dripping hair seem even scruffier.

"Who are you?" I asked, gripping Luna tightly.

"My name is Leander." He spoke with charm and civility, as if he were at a garden party, not clinging to a very small boat in a very large sea. "I'm pleased to meet you at long last, Niece."

I gaped at him. Even Luna looked up at this. Niece? That would make him our . . . uncle?

"You—you—" But I couldn't finish my thought. Symon called out, pointing, and we swung around to see that Manon's boat had come much closer. I let go of Luna and grabbed the ropes, pulling the sail taut.

Without another word, Leander slid off the *Cateline* and disappeared again into the waves. We caught the wind and surged forward as Manon advanced.

It was a race, like the one we had run with Manon's storm—a terrifying, heart-stopping race. If the sun went down completely before Manon caught up with us, there was a chance we could escape her, for we could sail in the dark with the help of the compass. As the sun set with agonizing deliberation, we sped along as fast as we could, but the black-winged boat gained on us swiftly. My heartbeat shook my whole body.

Luna had not taken her seat again. She cowered on the bottom of the boat, not speaking, refusing to meet my eyes. Darker the sky grew and closer Manon came. Then, when we could almost make out her form and features as she stood at the helm of her boat, the sun at last dropped below the western horizon. It pulled the last of its light down with it, as if an enormous candle had been extinguished.

The sudden darkness was disorienting. "Luna," Symon called in a low voice, "can you see the compass well enough?"

There was a pause, and then Luna answered softly, "Yes." In the gloom, I could see that she had climbed back onto her bench.

"Keep us on course. If we veer too far off, tell me."

"I will," Luna said. Her voice sounded very odd, and I longed to ask her what had happened. Had I been wrong, perhaps, and she'd not jumped but fallen overboard? Was she dizzy, or ill? I dared not speak, for I had no idea how near Manon's boat was, and I didn't want to make a noise that would tell her where we were.

We sailed silent and nearly blind. There was no sound but the faint slapping of waves against the side of the *Cateline*. We didn't know if Manon was close upon us or miles away. We couldn't tell how near we were to the third island, or if it might be Emmeline's island at all. We had no way to tell anything until the moon rose—and then, of course, Manon would be able to see us as well.

"The lutin called me 'niece,'" I whispered at last

to Symon, afraid my voice might carry too far on the night breeze.

"I heard," Symon replied, low. "What does it mean?"

"There was a part of our story . . . my mother's brother—," I began, then stopped. I had too many questions, and I was too tired and scared to make sense of it.

I shivered, for the wind was chill, and Symon most unexpectedly reached over and put a warm hand over mine. I stiffened for a moment, but soon I relaxed. After a few minutes he said, "Aurora, do you have a cloak in your bag?"

"I don't need it now," I told him softly, and he turned from me, removing his hand. Unable to see farther than the end of the batteau, I suddenly felt as if all my other senses were heightened. I could smell the fishy scent of the boat and the damp freshness of the wind. I heard the water shushing along the sides of the *Cateline* as it moved, and an occasional small splash as a fish leaped from the waves. On my lips I tasted sea salt—or was it the salt from the tears I'd wept when Luna was in the water? And my hand, where Symon had touched it, felt warmer than the rest of me.

"Luna!" Symon said. "Are we on course?"

Luna turned and replied, "We're fine. Just keep on." Her words were terse and strained.

"Sister, are you all right?" I asked her, concerned. "You're soaked and exhausted. Here, give me the compass for a time. It will keep me busy so I don't fall asleep. You can show me what to do and then take a rest."

"No!" Luna said vehemently. "It's my job, and I will do it."

She was so very stubborn.

On we sailed, more slowly now. Symon feared coming upon the third island unexpectedly and hitting rocks. We strained our eyes to peer through the darkness. And finally, the moon rose in the east, casting its pale glow on the waters.

We looked in every direction, but there was no sign of Manon, or the island, or the lutin. There was, in fact, no sign of anything at all. The *Cateline* glided over the waves toward an endless blank vista where water met sky, and in every direction we saw the same horizon.

"Have we lost her?" I asked, turning toward Symon.

"So it appears," he replied with relief. "Luna, check the map. How far away do you think we are from the island? Are we heading in the right direction?"

There was an uncomfortable silence. Then she cried out, "I don't know!"

Startled, I hissed, "Hush!"

"I don't need to hush," she said loudly. "How should I know how close we are, when I don't know how far it was to the island, or how fast we are going, or even how long we've been sailing?"

"But surely we should be near," Symon said reasonably. "Are you certain that we've stayed on course?"

Without warning, Luna let out a wail and burst into wild tears. Aghast, I scrambled up to her seat in the bow.

"Sister, what is it? Are you hurt? Oh please, tell me what's wrong." I folded her in my arms and held her, still damp and shaking with sobs. She was crying too hard to speak. "There, there," I said soothingly. "It will be all right. Everything will be fine, you'll see."

"No, it won't," Luna finally gulped, raising her head from my shoulder. "We are utterly lost. We are done for."

"It only seems that way," I assured her. "Truly, I believe we will find Emmeline. Don't despair!"

Luna hiccuped. "We'll never find her. We'll never get back or see Mama or Papa again. I'm sorry. I'm so sorry!"

I pulled back a little and looked closely at her. Her tear-filled eyes met mine, and I felt a sinking in the pit of my stomach. This was not just Luna being overly dramatic and hysterical. This was something serious.

"Luna, what did you do?" I tried to keep my voice level, though there was no way to make those words sound like anything other than an accusation. But Luna didn't bristle and grow angry. Instead, she shrank into herself, looking very defeated and frightened.

"Luna," I repeated. "Whatever did you do?"

"I dropped it into the ocean," she replied in a tiny voice.

"Dropped what?"

"The compass," she whispered. I stared at her.

"When—when did you drop it?" But I was afraid that I knew the answer.

"Before dark."

"But when, exactly?"

She began to cry again, shaking her head violently.

"What's happened?" Symon called.

It took me a minute to get the words out. "Luna has dropped the compass," I told him.

Symon winced. "Did it break?" he asked.

"She dropped it into the sea."

"Oh no," Symon breathed. "When? How long have we been sailing directionless?"

Luna did not answer.

"Luna, you must tell us," I insisted. "Stop your crying and tell us, now."

Luna took a deep, shuddering breath. "Since—since before sunset," she managed. "That's why I jumped in. I was trying to get it."

Symon let out one of his whistles. "But that was hours ago!" he exclaimed. "We could be anywhere. Anywhere at all."

"Oh please, please, forgive me," Luna begged, holding out her hands to Symon, though he was too far from her to reach. "I'm so very sorry. I shouldn't have pretended that I still had it."

Her words echoed in my ears—*I shouldn't have pretended*—and a sudden, unexpected rage took hold of me. I was so tired, and for the first time I wanted to blame my exhaustion—and everything else—on Luna. If she hadn't meddled, I wouldn't have pricked my finger. If she hadn't suggested we use the ladder, I wouldn't have fallen. If she hadn't dropped the compass, we wouldn't be hopelessly lost. I turned on her.

"You didn't pretend, you lied!" I cried, my voice shaking with fury. "Don't try to put a pretty name on it. You're always making trouble, and then you lie to protect yourself. And now your exploits have put us in the middle of the ocean, with no way to tell where we are and no way to get back home. We shall all die here because of you and your lies!"

There was a long, terrible silence. Almost immediately, I wished I could take back my angry words. When I thought of all that Luna had endured for me, I was ashamed. She had suffered through battering by sea and wind, through hunger and thirst and heat and exhaustion. She had nearly died—most horribly—in quicksand, all for my sake. But what was said could not be unsaid.

Symon, ever practical, acted as though I hadn't spoken. "Well, I shall have to try to steer by the stars." His voice was matter-of-fact.

"Can I help?" I asked humbly. I would apologize later. I would make it up to her somehow.

"Maybe," Symon said. "Tell me, do you see the North Star?"

I scanned the clear night sky. It looked like there were a thousand stars, or a million, all clustered together.

"It should be at the end of the tail of the constellation Ursa Minor, the Little Bear."

Though it seemed very long ago, I remembered standing outside Castle Armelle with Luna as Master Julien pointed out the constellations. Cetus the whale, Delphinus the dolphin, Sagittarius the Archer. Where had he said Ursa Minor was? I strained to see the shape of a bear in the sky. "That one, I think," I said at last, pointing at a group of stars. "The North Star is the brightest one, at the tip of the bear's tail—is that right?"

Symon, looking upward where I pointed, nodded. "If that's north, then we want to head slightly to the left. That is, if we're still on course."

"Shouldn't we go back?" I asked anxiously. "How can we ever find one tiny island in the whole dark sea without a compass?"

"If we go back, we're certain to fail," Symon noted. "If we go on, we have at least a chance of succeeding. And besides, Manon is surely between us and the mainland."

I took a deep, shaky breath and reached out to put a hand over Symon's, as he had done before to me. "I'm sorry," I said. "I never meant to put you in such danger."

"Oh, I knew it wouldn't be easy," he said calmly, turning up his palm and twining his fingers with mine. "And think of the stories I'll be able to tell when we return!" He gave me his crooked grin, and I pulled my hand back, feeling my cheeks flush.

I kept hold of the ropes and tried to attend to the stars, and we turned slightly to adjust our course. "Keep watch, Luna," Symon said. "We'll need your keen eyes." His voice was very kind. Luna, huddled in the bow, nodded wordlessly.

The night seemed to last forever. My back and arms throbbed from sitting upright so long and holding tightly to the ropes, and I fought Sleep with every breath. Luna and Symon took turns resting and holding the tiller. We ate most of our remaining food.

There was no way to make tea, so I sprinkled the little bit of devil's shrub left in the vial into my last ration of fresh water. The mixture was gritty and tasted awful, but I knew that without it, I was finished. Indeed, with no more water, we all were.

The moon set, and then clouds came in and blotted out the stars. The breeze stiffened, and I needed all my strength to hold the sail steady. The waves slapped more loudly against the boat.

As the sky began to lighten in the east, Luna sat up straight and pointed. "Is that land?" she called out.

We peered through the dimness. I could make out a dark form, a small hillock rising from the sea.

"It's too small to be the island on the map," Symon said, "but we'll head for it. Perhaps there's a spring, or at least a pool of rainwater, and we can drink."

We turned toward the knoll and approached it swiftly. As we neared, Luna said, "I see two islands now. No, wait, there are three!"

The sky turned from dark to light gray as the sun rose behind the clouds, and in the first light we could see what Luna saw. Three brown humps, one behind the other, all the same size.

"Those are very odd-looking islands," Symon remarked uneasily.

And then they moved.

I gasped. "Oh, what are they?" I cried.

Symon swung the tiller, and I ducked as the boom came about. But before the boat turned completely, a fourth island erupted from the sea, closer to us. Only it was not an island—it was a head. A serpent's head, with a jaw twice the size of the *Cateline* and a pair of dark, fathomless eyes that fixed on us as the boat spun around and we prepared to flee.

Up and up it rose, seawater cascading from its scales and splashing into the ocean. Its neck seemed to stretch to the sky, and it opened its enormous mouth as if to swallow us with a single gulp. Luna gave a wild shriek, and even Symon cried out, but I was too terrified to scream.

"The map was right," I whispered. "Here be dragons."

Of a Threat from Three Directions

The *Cateline* swung around, and then we were speeding over the water away from the sea-dragon, faster than we had ever gone before. We skimmed across the waves as the wind blew harder and harder, with a terrible sulfurous smell that made us cough and choke.

I glanced back and saw the monster rear up in the water, its head so high that it seemed to tower directly over us, though it was still a hundred yards away. Its scales were brownish-green, and its neck as thick around as the biggest oak in our forest. On its head spikes erupted in all directions, and it had nostrils that flared and teeth as long as branches, but sharp.

That was not the worst of it, though. When I turned to face front again, I saw a black sail in the distance moving toward us.

"It's Manon's boat!" I shouted. Symon pulled at the tiller and we veered swiftly to the right. Now we sailed at an angle as the sea-dragon approached from one side and Manon from the other. The acrid breath of the dragon whipped the waves into whitecaps, and I heard a roaring sound. I feared it was the noise of my own blood rushing through me and that I would faint. As we skipped wildly across the ocean, the sound grew louder and louder, and suddenly I understood its source.

Directly in front of us, the water rotated in a circle to a center that appeared like a great, white-foaming hole in the sea. There was no way to avoid it.

"Whirlpool!" Symon yelled, just an instant before the boat was caught in its deadly current. We were at the outermost rim. Our movement as we rotated seemed terribly slow, after our great speed just moments before. But the spiraling vortex pulled us steadily in. Our next circuit was faster, and the next faster still. In a great panic I worked the ropes of the sail as Symon struggled furiously with the tiller. It was no use. Faster and faster we spun, the world revolving before my eyes.

I saw the serpent pass by, then the black sail of Manon's boat, then the serpent again as we turned, ever closer to the hole in the center. Serpent, sail; serpentsailserpentsail.

Through my dizzy dread, I remembered the cruel things I'd said to Luna. I couldn't bear it if they were the last words she ever heard from me. "Forgive me, Sister!" I cried out, just before the boat reached the center of the whirlpool. With a great sucking noise, the water pulled us below the surface, and we were gone.

Everything seemed to slow to a crawl. I saw Luna's terrified face and reached for her, but she floated out of my grasp amid the shattered debris of Symon's boat.

And then I saw something strange beyond all reckoning. The lutin, Leander, swam up behind Luna and took hold of her beneath the waves. I blinked my eyes hard, for the salt stung them, but when I opened them again, he was still there. He held my sister with one hand. Symon clutched the lutin's shoulder, his own eyes wide with bewilderment.

Leander pointed to me and then to Luna. I kicked my legs hard and moved near enough to grab her arm. Then he motioned to his own chest and his mouth, and it seemed that he was telling me to breathe. My lungs ached for air, but I knew that if I tried to inhale, I would take in water and suffocate. Of course the lutin could breathe like a fish. But I could not. Still, it was impossible to hold my breath any longer. I let out the air I had been holding and drew in a breath, prepared to choke.

I did not choke. My lungs filled, and I gasped and breathed again. The others' chests were heaving too, and I realized that we were all breathing below the surface of the sea. It was incredible, but it was happening.

Leander pointed the way ahead and began to swim like a dolphin, as I'd seen him do before. I kept my grip tight on Luna and kicked my legs, and the others kicked too, and paddled with their free hands. We were clumsy compared to the lutin, but we moved forward, swimming down into darkness.

I could barely see Luna's arm where my hand grasped her, it was so dark. But then a bluish light moved toward us out of the murky depths. As it passed close by, I saw it was a bizarre-looking fish with bulging eyes and a sort of lantern affixed to its head. The lantern was giving off the blue light. Other similar fish emerged from the darkness and then disappeared again. Once I glimpsed a row of glowing blue dots, and then as we came closer I could make out a long, thin fish spotted with blue. A horrid phosphorescent snakelike creature scared me with a show of teeth, but it slithered into a cave between two rocks and didn't bother us.

As we moved upward from the depths, daylight pierced the water enough for us to see more clearly. We swam through what looked like a forest of strange white branches that waved in the gentle current. Here, the fish were small and beautifully colored—bright blue, orange, yellow. Some were striped, others spotted, still others decorated with swirls of pink or green. They darted around us, above us, and below us, and I swiveled my head to try to see them all. My fear had left me completely, and I was all amazement.

Suddenly we swam into a cloud of tiny silver fish, so thick that I couldn't see anything else. I clutched Luna tightly and tried to call her name, but my voice came out in a stream of bubbles. The fish surged in a circle and then were gone, and behind them came a huge turtle, flapping its winglike fins as if it were a bird flying slowly through the water. It was ridiculous and elegant at the same time, moving with such ease that it seemed completely unrelated to the awkward land turtle I'd seen in the woods near our palace.

We passed through the underwater forest and into a dim tunnel. Blue-green sparks danced off our bodies as we swam. I trailed my hand through the water, marveling at the way the light seemed to cling to it. We were our own lanterns now. I saw my expression of astonishment mirrored in the faces of the others.

The tunnel slanted upward, and at the top was the sparkle and gleam of sunlight. At last we rose to the surface, gasping in the rich air. The waves pushed us toward a glistening beach and tumbled us onto white sand, where we lay panting.

I rose to my knees and looked around. The sands ended in a field of flowers in a hundred strange shapes and colors. Tiny birds with wings that beat too fast to see and butterflies as vivid as the fish we'd swum beside flitted among them. The songs of other, unseen birds filled the air. The breeze was fragrant with a scent like Mama's perfume.

"Oh," I breathed in awe. It was so different from the stark, craggy landscape of our seaside cliffs and the shaded green of our forest. The lovely warmth, though, brought on a wave of tiredness, and I remembered with sudden alarm that I had no more devil's shrub to keep me awake.

There was a stirring behind me, and I turned. Leander sat in the sand, leaning back on his hands. His clothing was luxurious, made of velvet and silk, and his long, dark hair waved over his collar. He didn't even appear to be wet, though he'd just emerged from the sea.

Beside me, Luna struggled to her feet. "Who *are* you?" she challenged him.

He laughed at her belligerence. "I am Leander, Princess. Your uncle Leander. I am very pleased to meet you properly—though we did meet before, when you dove into the waves."

She narrowed her eyes. "You're our mother's brother? The one who disappeared?"

"I am."

"Why did you never come back? You broke your parents' hearts!" Luna cried.

For the first time, Leander's nonchalant smile faltered. "I had to disappear," he said. "Manon was set on destroying me. She might have harmed my family, too—your grandparents, your mother. You cannot know what I sacrificed when I left, Niece."

"But . . . could this be true?" Luna asked me.

I tried to remember our mother's exact words. "Mama never told us her brother's name. It could well have been Leander."

She turned back to Leander. "So you were once a prince, and then you became an imp?"

He laughed again, his good humor restored. "I prefer not to use the word *imp*. Imps are nasty, brutish creatures. I am a lutin by choice—and it's lucky for you that I chose to be one!"

I got to my feet, trying to comb my fingers through my dripping hair and adjust my dress, soaked and torn at hem and sleeve.

"You've been following us, haven't you?" I asked.

"Indeed I have," Prince Leander said. "You have had some fine adventures, I must say! But you have been very resourceful, you and your sister."

"Resourceful?" Luna repeated, puzzled.

"Your pine pitch idea, when you were approaching Melusine—that was truly a stroke of genius."

I could see that Luna liked the praise. To my surprise, though, she admitted, "That wasn't my idea. It was Aurora's."

"Ah," the prince said, raising an eyebrow. "Nevertheless, it was a shrewd scheme. The two of you managed it very nicely. You work well together. And you, sir"—this was to Symon—"you are truly a master with sail and tiller!" The tips of Symon's ears turned red as he scuffed his boot in the sand.

"Wait," Luna said, her hands on her hips. "You were there? At Melusine's Isle?"

"For a time," he answered. "I swam beneath your boat and kept you from the rocks."

That annoyed her. "Well, why didn't you simply turn us?" she asked. "Or keep us from Melusine altogether?"

"I would never have let her harm you, dearest niece!" he said. "But, you see, I feared Manon might be watching. I did not want to reveal myself unless I had to. Your cleverness made that unnecessary. And is it not significant that you escaped from the Siren yourselves?"

Luna blinked in confusion. "What do you mean?" she demanded. But Leander only smiled.

"And you helped us to breathe below the water?" I asked him.

"It is one of my small talents," he said modestly. "As long as you were touching me, or touching one who touched me, you could breathe as a fish does."

"But you didn't rescue us on the Island of Beasts," Luna accused.

"No, I am only truly useful in water and air," he said. "And again, you did not need my help there. You saved yourselves. Besides, the quicksand would have ruined my silk waistcoat."

What a strange creature Leander was! So calm, so unruffled, so . . . not quite human. But I thought of what he'd said: *You cannot know what I sacrificed when I left, Niece.* Though his tone had been composed, the words told me that he had suffered.

Luna contemplated him for a moment and said, "Well, I'm pleased to meet you, too, Uncle—even though I didn't know you existed a week ago." She too had decided to accept him.

Then Leander's face brightened and he rose from the sand, brushing off his fine clothing. "Ah, here comes our host," he said.

We turned to see a woman walking toward us. She was small and shapely, very pretty—no, she was beautiful. Her lips were rosy and her eyes deep blue. Her dark hair cascaded over her shoulders to her waist. She was dressed in a gossamer gown of pale blue cinched with a darker blue sash, and her feet—like Luna's—were bare.

"Princesses," said Prince Leander, in a tone of pride and accomplishment, "meet your great-great-god-mother Emmeline."

Of an Island Out of Time

We stared at the woman in bewilderment. She must have been nearly two centuries old, but she looked no more than twenty. With a smile on her lovely face, she walked straight to me and took my hands. Her touch was warm and gentle.

"You left off a *great*," she said to Prince Leander, and laughed, sounding like the wind chimes in our kitchen garden.

"Emmeline?" I asked uncertainly.

"Yes, dearest—at last! I have so longed to meet you,

Aurora. Oh, you are as beautiful as your mother!"

"But—," Luna sputtered. "But you don't look old!"

"Luna!" I protested.

"And this is Luna," Emmeline said, unoffended. "Sweet child! Let me look at you." She released my hands and cupped Luna's face. "Why, the short hair suits you perfectly! But to cut it with a piece of glass . . ."

"How—," Luna began.

Emmeline brushed Luna's curls back from her face. "I have watched everything, my darlings. You've faced such dangers! It is a testament to your strength of purpose that you have done so well."

"It wasn't only our strength, but Symon's, and Prince—Uncle—Leander's," I corrected her. "Without them we would surely have died."

"You did well, lad," Emmeline said to Symon, and again he blushed. "And Leander! I set him a task—to find you and bring you to me. And I see he has succeeded."

"I am at your service, milady, as always," Leander said.

She reached out a hand, and he grasped it and brought it to his lips. Emmeline gave him a little half curtsy, and he bowed low to her, as if they were at a dance. Luna and I exchanged a grin at their funny little pantomime. Then, despite my joy at having found

Emmeline at last, I couldn't help yawning hugely. "You need tea," Luna said immediately.

"The vial is empty," I told her.

"Oh no!" She turned to Emmeline. "You must help Aurora," she demanded. "She's been awake for days, and now we're out of devil's shrub. Surely you have a potion or an enchantment that will work."

Emmeline's smooth brow creased with worry. "I have been working on something," she said. "I do not know how much it will help. Let us go to my house, and I will prepare it for you. And you can have baths and fresh clothes and something good to eat."

Emmeline took my hand and Luna's, and we started up the path, disturbing a flock of rainbow-colored birds as we brushed through the flowers.

"If you've been watching us—through magic, I suppose—have you seen Mama?" I asked her. "Is she all right? Is she well?"

"Not well, but managing," Emmeline said. "She knows of your quest. Your father has sent out ships, of course, but they will not find us here."

Not well, but managing. That was better than I'd feared. I wondered, then, if the sense of being watched I'd felt since we left home had been caused by Emmeline's magic. But that feeling had been very dark and chilling. I couldn't imagine that Emmeline would have caused it.

"Did you send Leander to keep us safe from Manon?" Luna asked. Her eyes were bright with curiosity.

Emmeline sighed. "Yes, dearest. I could not help you myself. Manon detests your mother, you, your sister—and especially me. She was so angry that I won Leander's heart, and then when I changed your mother's curse from death to a hundred years of sleep . . . well, she has sought revenge ever since. She would have destroyed me if she had found me. She is much stronger than I."

I thought of the black sail that had been so close before the whirlpool sucked us down. "She was right behind us," I said. "She may have followed us." I turned and eyed the water anxiously.

Emmeline nodded, unsurprised. "Yes, she was close. But she will have to find her way here, and you know that is not easy. We have a little time yet."

Luna could not stop chattering. "But what is this place? And how are you so young, Great-Great-Great-Godmother?" she persisted.

Prince Leander, walking behind us with Symon, chuckled. "A fairy's exterior reflects her interior," he said. "Emmeline is as beautiful as she is good."

"Oh, stop!" Emmeline protested. "Really, it is mostly an illusion. I am as old as . . . well, I am very old indeed." But it was impossible to believe, looking at her, just as it was incredible to imagine that Prince

Leander too was ancient.

"And this island is a place out of time, just a little," Emmeline went on. "The only way here is through the whirlpool, and the whirlpool is always changing position."

"You conjured the whirlpool yourself?" Surely a fairy who could do that would be able to save me!

"It was rather difficult," Emmeline admitted humbly. "It took me a very long time."

"It's a wonder we found it, out in the middle of the sea," Symon remarked.

Emmeline's wind-chime laugh bubbled out. "Not a wonder at all, Captain! It was entirely on purpose."

"What do you mean?" Luna asked.

"The sea-dragon—he was mine. I am very proud of him. He pushed you toward the whirlpool, just as I had planned."

Luna's expression was both amazed and angry. I could understand why—that dragon had terrified us. "So we were never really in danger?" she asked. "I was so frightened!"

"Well . . . ," Emmeline replied cautiously, "I am not entirely certain. A dragon is a difficult thing to control."

"But if you can summon a dragon, Godmother, surely you can remove the curse from Aurora—can't you?"

Emmeline sighed again. "I have worked very hard to do that. Since the moment Manon proclaimed the curse, I have been trying. I do not think I have the power. Still, I shall attempt it."

The path widened then and became a gravel lane lined with tall, fernlike trees. At its end stood a white stone house, grand but not imposing. It was welcoming, with bright blue shutters on its long windows and flower beds bordering the front. Peacocks strode on the grass, stopping now and then to shriek and raise their turquoise tails like fans.

Luna was enthralled. She had once seen a picture of a peacock in a book, and for months she had begged Papa to bring us one, but he insisted that their harsh cries would be too disturbing for Mama. Now she darted onto the green grass toward the nearest bird.

"Wait, Luna!" Emmeline warned her.

But Luna, being Luna, ignored her and reached out to pet the bird. Immediately it stretched its long neck and nipped her, hard.

"It *bit* me!" Luna cried. "I'm bleeding!"

Symon, struggling to hide a smile, ran forward to shoo the peacock away, and it turned on him fiercely. He and Luna retreated as quickly as they could, but when their feet hit the gravel of the path, they both tripped and fell on their backsides. We three—Prince Leander, Emmeline, and I—burst out laughing as they curled into balls to protect themselves from the bird's furious pecking.

"Help! It will kill us!" Luna howled. Emmeline stopped laughing long enough to speak a word that caused the irate bird to turn and stalk stiff-legged back onto the lawn.

"It isn't *that* funny," Luna said, standing to brush the gravel from her clothes, but even she had to giggle as another peacock came near Symon and he stiffened, ready to run.

"You don't fear dragons or the Beasts of Gevadan, but a peacock—now that's a formidable foe!" I teased them as we reached the door of the house.

Inside, it was just as beautiful as outside. The rooms were filled with light, their windows framed with gauzy white curtains that floated in the warm breezes. The walls were the lightest pastel colors, bare of artwork, but the ceiling of the entryway was painted with the myth of Apollo and Daphne: the nymph, escaping from Apollo, turning into a tree as she flees.

"First," Emmeline said, "we must try to help Aurora. Come with me."

We all followed her to a small sitting room with tall glass doors that opened onto a garden. On this ceiling Rapunzel leaned from her tower, her long golden braid reaching nearly to the ground.

Emmeline pointed to a bell that hung by the doors and said, "That bell is my warning signal. If anything comes through the whirlpool, it will sound."

Anything meant Manon, of course, and we grew silent. Then Luna asked, "Did it ring when we came?"

"It did," Emmeline replied. "That is how I knew you were here. Though I had been watching you, so I expected you."

Then she beckoned to me. "Come over here, darling." We stood in front of a table that held a tray with a small pot and a spoon on it. The pot was made of shimmering mother-of-pearl.

"Are you going to cast a spell? Don't you need a wand?" Luna asked.

Emmeline smiled. "Wands are really just for show. We do not often use them." She took up the tiny spoon and dipped it in the pot. Then she chanted something in a low, musical voice, and sprinkled her potion over me. It had a marvelous smell, like lavender and rosemary and something a little darker. I breathed in deeply. A tremor passed through me. Suddenly I was awake, truly awake, as I hadn't been for days and days. Then I sneezed violently, and all at once I was as tired as I had been before.

"Oh, Godmother!" I exclaimed. "For just an instant . . . oh, do try it again!"

"It is not strong enough," she mourned.

"Try it again!" Luna pleaded, and Symon said, "Yes, please do!"

Once more, Emmeline sprinkled me with the powder, and I woke, and sneezed, and was tired. At Luna's insistence she did it a third time, but the result was the same.

"I am so sorry, child," Emmeline said. "I am just not skilled enough."

Luna stamped her foot. "Why not?" she demanded. "You're a fairy, are you not? Why is Manon stronger than you?"

"She always has been," Emmeline admitted. "I believe it is because I have some human blood in me, from far back. I cannot help it, though I wish I could— oh, more than anything!"

I was utterly discouraged. For a moment I'd thought that it would work. To have had that hope and then have it dashed . . .

"I have other possibilities," my great-great-great-godmother said reassuringly. But I no longer had much confidence in her. I blinked back tears.

"Leander and I will keep working." Emmeline patted my hand. "We just need a little time." But I could tell from her expression that she knew we didn't have much time. Manon was coming. We would have to face her whether we were ready or not.

Luna linked her arm in mine, and we all left the sitting room and trudged up a long staircase behind Emmeline. We separated from Symon and Leander at the top, and Emmeline took Luna and me into a room where an enormous copper tub awaited us. I glanced up to see what art graced this ceiling, and gasped. The painting depicted a girl sitting at a spinning wheel, her finger pierced by the spindle and a drop of scarlet blood caught in mid-fall.

"Is that Mama?" I whispered.

Emmeline looked up, and her face fell. "Oh, darling, I'm sorry!" she exclaimed. "I'd quite forgotten that was here. I just . . . well, I like to remember my favorite people and stories, and I . . . shall I move the bath? Or remove the painting?"

Luna stared at the ceiling. "Remove the painting?" she repeated. "Wouldn't that be a lot of work?"

"It's beautiful," I said. "But she looks like Luna, not like me." I had to turn my eyes away, for suddenly I missed Mama—and Papa too, and Castle Armelle— with an almost painful longing.

"She had your lovely hair when she was young," Emmeline said, "but she had Luna's smile, and Luna's fearless spirit."

"Our mother?" I said, disbelieving. I thought of

Mama's delicacy, her pale face, her fainting spells. Luna's spirit?

"Ah, that was long, long ago," Emmeline said. "Before her troubles began."

The door to the room opened then, and—I don't know how else to describe it—a jug full of steaming water came in. No one carried it; it seemed to float in midair all on its own. It emptied itself into the tub as Luna and I watched, openmouthed. Behind it came another jug, and another and another, and they poured themselves until the tub was full.

Emmeline laughed at our expressions. "It is much harder to produce the actual servants," she said. "All I really need is the service, which I can create easily. So my servants do not truly exist, but their work gets done."

In the warm bath, Sleep again threatened to overwhelm me, and I pinched the inside of my arm hard to rouse myself. The tub was big enough for us both, and Luna washed my hair and I scrubbed her short curls as Emmeline explained how she knew Prince Leander. Some of what she told us echoed what we'd learned from Mama and Papa, but some of it was new.

"We met at your mother's christening," she said. "But Manon believed he was hers."

I remembered Mama describing this. "She was in love with him."

"Desperately," Emmeline said. "She loved him, and she wanted to be his forever."

"But she's horrible!" Luna said. "Of course he could never love her."

"Manon is younger than I, you know," Emmeline pointed out. "She was not so horrible then. In fact, she was quite beautiful—though it was a beauty with a dangerous edge. She and Leander had known each other for quite a while. They had spent some time together, and she had convinced herself that her feelings for him were returned. But then he saw me, and I saw him. . . ." Her voice trailed off.

"And then?" Luna prompted.

"Manon could not contain her fury. I believe she went a little mad. She pronounced her curse on your mother, and I modified it, to the best of my ability. And then we fled, Leander and I.

"He took me away, and we spent some time on a lovely tropical isle before Manon discovered us. She imprisoned him and kept him captive for years."

I thought of the story Symon had told about the lutin trapped in a cave. So it was true, and it had been my uncle! How would such a fate change a man? I wondered. To be alone so long, to lose one's family . . .

Emmeline went on. "I looked everywhere, followed every hint or rumor I heard. Then when I came to him at last, I could not set him free—I did not have the power. But I learned that I could turn him into a lutin and give him the power to free himself.

"Finally we found this little sandbar in the sea. It has been our hiding place. I made it as much like that other isle as I could—the plants, the birds, the warmth. Ah, but I loved it there!"

Her face was open and dreamy, and it was clear that what she really loved in those memories was Leander.

"Now," Emmeline said as we dried ourselves with towels that floated across the room to us, "what would you like to wear? Luna, do you want leggings and a tunic or a dress?"

"I suppose I could wear a dress," Luna mused, to my surprise. "Do you have one that's green? Leaf green?"

"No peacock blue?" I teased, and she made a face at me and then laughed.

"I think we can manage leaf green," Emmeline assured her. "And for you, Aurora—lilac, I think." She threw open the doors of a large wardrobe that stood against the wall and pulled out two dresses, flowing gowns with simple lines. There were no tight bodices to pinch us, no ruffles, no heavy embroidery or jewels. They were like wearing air, as unlike the dresses we wore at home as could be, and they fit us perfectly. Emmeline placed a circlet of emeralds around Luna's curls and one of amethysts on my head, and gave us soft slippers dyed to match.

"Now you look like princesses again!" she exclaimed, clapping her hands with pleasure.

"But there's no mirror," I complained.

"No, I do not keep mirrors," Emmeline said. "A mirror would reflect me as I truly am—wrinkles, warts, and all. I much prefer the image you see." It was impossible to imagine a version of Emmeline that was old and wrinkled and warty, as beautiful as she seemed.

We went down to dinner, descending the stairs to the admiring gazes of Prince Leander and Symon, who waited for us below. Symon too was clean and well-dressed in clothes that looked elegant but comfortable. He was very handsome with his hair brushed and his face washed; very handsome indeed.

When Prince Leander raised my hand and kissed it, I curtsied, but I had to hold back a smile at Symon's red-faced stammer and awkward bow as he approached me.

"I'm just your deckhand, the same as ever," I whispered. Startled, he laughed and looked himself again.

We sat at a long table inlaid with a mosaic of shells. Above us, in the flickering candlelight from a pink coral chandelier, a ceiling fresco showed ancient gods and goddesses feasting. Our dinner came to us as our bathwater had: first the soup tureen appeared, then a platter of meats, and finally a sweet, all moving to the table as if carried by invisible hands. We served ourselves, for as Emmeline explained, "The dishes are only aloft because I concentrate on them. If I took my attention from the bowl for even an instant, the soup would be in your lap!"

The meal was delicious and merry, though waves of drowsiness hit me between each course. The very last of the devil's shrub had worn off completely. I knew I couldn't stay awake much longer. I tried to memorize everything: the taste of the food, the feel of the soft fabric of my dress, my sister's dear face. I didn't want to lose it all, and I fought as hard as I could. I wet my napkin with water and dabbed my face; I pinched my arms and legs. Luna saw my distress and kicked me gently under the table now and then, rousing me. Her expression was troubled, and I was grateful for her concern.

When the table had cleared itself, Emmeline and Leander left us to walk briefly in the garden. "We shan't be gone long," my great-great-great-godmother said. "I want to practice my spells one last time." *One last time.* The words made me shiver.

Luna noticed and said, "Sister, it's better that we face Manon than that we keep running from her."

"Is it?" I asked hopelessly.

"I think so." She sounded very unhappy, and I reached out and hugged her. She clung to me.

"Yes, you're right," I said. "I'm almost as tired of being afraid as I am just plain tired."

Luna let me go then and staggered upstairs to sleep, her first real chance at rest in days. Symon, however, refused to leave me. "I'll stay awake with you," he insisted.

I looked at him and saw the blue shadows under his eyes. "You must rest," I told him. "You may need your strength later. I'll be all right. I don't think lutins and fairies sleep—I'll go out to the garden with them."

He hesitated, but then he gave such an enormous yawn that he had to laugh and agree. Lingering for a few minutes, he asked, "Your godmother and your uncle—they're a strange couple, aren't they?"

"Actually, I think they're very well-suited. They are both—well, both a little . . ." I trailed off, not sure what I meant. Odd? Remarkable?

"Aye, I see what you mean," Symon said, grinning. "They are well-matched. As you and I are, don't you think?"

I thought he was teasing, but I wasn't certain. "We're far too young to think of such things," I said hesitantly. "Besides, I am a princess, and you are . . ."

"A smelly fisherman?" he finished for me, raising an eyebrow.

"No, no! That wasn't what I meant at all!" I exclaimed. I thought of all that Symon had done with us and for us over the past days. "You've been so brave—so wonderful. We would never have gotten this far without you. I'm so very grateful. . . ."

"It's been an adventure," Symon allowed. "And I'm grateful too."

"For what?" I was baffled. "Your boat is destroyed, and we're stuck here on an island with no way to return. And even if we do find our way back—"

"I'm grateful you gave me the chance to go," Symon said seriously. "My whole life was just fishing before—trying to catch enough to get through each winter, so that the next summer I could catch enough again. I love the sea, and now that I've seen beyond Vittray and my little strand, I want to see more. Oh, Aurora, I want to see everything!" He grasped my hand in his excitement at the thought.

"I hope you will," I said softly. "I hope we get back."

"We will," he said with great confidence. "And when we do, I plan to visit you sometimes, though you are a princess, and I just a fisherman."

My face grew warm. "If Papa allows it," I said.

"Well," Symon said, "you could tell him to allow it.

You will be queen someday, after all."

I was starting to feel quite flustered. "What I meant was, Papa probably has some prince or other in mind to court me."

"I don't recall mentioning courting you," Symon said with a wicked smile. "And I may never be a prince, but I don't think I will always be a fisherman."

By now I was completely confounded. Before I could stop myself, I spoke, so rudely that I was shocked at my own words. "No? Have you plans to go into business and raise a great fortune and acquire a title and come calling on me when we are both grown?"

He was not the least bit insulted, but only laughed. "That's a very interesting idea," he remarked, moving closer to me. He bent his head, and without thinking I raised my face, and he kissed me. His lips were soft and sweet. Their touch made me dizzy with happiness.

He went off to bed then with many backward glances, and I watched him go, feeling the heat in my cheeks and the pounding of my heart. The memory of that kiss would help keep me awake for hours, I was sure.

As the moon rose I wandered through the grounds, looking for Emmeline and Prince Leander. Strange and exotic plants surrounded a pool at the very center of the garden, and I drew closer to splash some water on my face and rouse myself. I sat on the edge and looked in. My own reflection looked back, a pale girl with a dreamy smile and tired, dark-circled eyes.

Then, oddly, as I stared into the pool, I began to see other places in the water. I could make out the beach where we had met Emmeline, and the hallway of her house. I saw Emmeline herself walking in the meadow under the moonlight, hand in hand with Prince Leander as they talked intently. So this was how she had watched us, as we sailed over the seas in search of her!

The visions faded, and I saw my reflection again. But as I looked, my face in the water seemed to change. My mirrored eyes closed, though my real eyes were still open. And then I saw Luna in the reflection and spun around to see if she was behind me. She was not. I turned back. In the pool's image she stood in a room I didn't recognize. Her face appeared older and sadder, and I saw that she held a babe in her arms. As I watched, the babe lengthened and grew, and then it stood by her side and she held a second child.

I saw my parents in another room, the conservatory of our castle. Their forlorn faces changed and aged under my gaze, wrinkles and creases appearing and spreading. At last their own eyes closed, and their cheeks grew as pale as marble. I realized I was looking at their deaths. The reflected Luna aged too as

I watched. Her eyes closed and her skin took on the translucence of death. I felt hot tears on my cheeks. It was heartbreaking, and I pulled away, crying, "No!"

"Aurora!" I heard Emmeline call as she ran toward me. "Do not look in the pool!" But it was too late.

I stood, trembling and weeping, and my godmother took me in her arms, stroking my hair. "They are all dead!" I sobbed.

"No, no," Emmeline murmured. "When the pool shows the future, it only reveals what *might* happen, not what will happen."

"But . . . what was I seeing? When might that happen?" I managed.

"If you fell asleep," Emmeline said gently, voicing what I already knew. "If you slept for a hundred years."

I had seen my parents' sad lives, Luna's sorrowful motherhood, all occurring without me. I nodded, wiping my eyes with my hand. "I won't fall asleep," I vowed. "It will not happen."

And then a sound shattered the quiet of the night, a peal of noise that made us both jump in fright. Again it sounded, and yet again. It was the frantic tolling of a bell, the signal that I dreaded: Manon had arrived.

16

Of Sorcery and Sudden Sleep

The bell rang and rang, and I stood in shock, unable to move. A wave of airless cold blew across my face as Emmeline led me back through the garden to the house. "It will be all right," she said to me. But I didn't believe her, for I felt that she didn't quite believe herself.

Luna and Symon clattered down the stairs a few moments later, bleary-eyed. Luna was dressed in her tunic and leggings again. "She's here!" my sister exclaimed, and I nodded. She took my icy hands in hers.

"I can feel her," I whispered. "I felt her in the forest, and in Vittray, and even on the sea. She pulls at me, she and her servant Sleep."

"I won't let you go," Luna said fiercely. "I'll pinch you and prod you and yank your hair to keep you awake. She will never have you!" I laughed shakily and squeezed her hand, knowing that she meant every word.

"We will go down to the shore to meet her," Emmeline instructed, her voice calm. "I cannot face her and keep all this intact as well." She motioned to the house around us, and I wondered how much of it was really there and how much only imagined. The table and chairs had felt real, and the food had tasted good. It all looked very solid and true.

But there was no time for such thoughts. We walked quickly down the path and through the moonlit meadow. Emmeline led with Prince Leander, then Symon and Luna and I walked together.

As we neared the beach, we could make out the tall mast and limp black sail of Manon's boat, which rested on the sand. Somehow the vessel had survived the whirlpool intact. There was no crew that I could see. Only one figure stood on the strand, her dark cape billowing in the breeze.

Then we lined up, the five of us facing her. Symon was on one side of me, and Luna was on the other.

Manon threw back her hood, and my eyes widened in surprise as I saw her closely. She didn't look at all like the crone we'd seen on the pier at Vittray. Her face was young and beautiful, her skin white as the whitest sand, her eyes and brows and hair sable black. But in her malicious eyes and the cruel slash of her mouth, I could make out traces of the old woman I'd watched as we sailed away, and I knew it was truly she who stood before us.

"At last we meet again," Manon said. Her voice was deep and throaty. She was gazing at Emmeline and Prince Leander, not at me.

Leander bowed. "You look very well, Manon," he said, his tone serene. But his jaunty smile was gone.

Manon scowled. "I would look far better if I had spent the last century as I should have—with you. The two of us, joyful together. Instead, I have been shaped by great sorrow and loss."

"You are shaped by cruelty and revenge," Emmeline countered, stepping forward. "You could not have kept him, you know. He loved only me."

Even in the moonlight, I could see Manon's eyes flash. "You are wrong. He loved me once. It was your magic that took him from me. He never would have left me otherwise."

"My magic?" Emmeline repeated. "Am I so very good

at magic? Then we have nothing to fear from you." She laughed, as if to show her unconcern, but she sounded strained. I exchanged an anxious glance with Symon.

"You are less than nothing," Manon said harshly to Emmeline. "You are as a splinter in my finger. I will pull you out and toss you away."

"I am not quite as foolish as I was, nor as weak," Emmeline retorted. "I have had some years to perfect my skills."

"Perfect them?" Manon mocked her. "Do you mean this—this illusion?" She swept an arm around in a circle. As her arm moved, the parts of the island that she pointed to wavered and then disappeared. With dread I watched as the meadow, the trees behind, and the land beneath vanished. In a moment, there was nothing left but the strand we stood upon, a narrow beach in a great dark sea.

I could not stop from crying out fearfully, and Manon turned her attention to me.

"So, my dear," she remarked. "You have managed to resist Sleep all this time! You are very clever, very clever indeed." Manon's gaze felt unbearably heavy, and I wobbled and would have fallen to my knees if Symon's grip had not kept me upright.

"It is harder when I am near, is it not?" Manon went on. "Imagine what would happen if I were just to reach out and touch you! Could you stay awake then, do you think?"

I moaned as Manon's hand came closer and closer to me. I felt paralyzed. I tried to make my legs move, but they didn't obey me. Was it fear or magic that held me in place? I couldn't tell.

But then Emmeline stepped between us. "I will not let you," she declared.

"Ah, good," Manon said, sounding pleased. "I have been waiting—come, let us see your power!"

Emmeline hesitated, then spoke a string of words I didn't recognize. Not Latin, of that I was certain. The force of the incantation pushed Manon backward a few steps, and seawater splashed the hem of her dress.

"Surely you can do better than that," Manon taunted. She uttered her own spell in what sounded like the same language. Emmeline was lifted off her feet as if by invisible hands and tossed off the strand, landing ankle-deep in the sea.

It was like watching a horrific game of lawn tennis, as the incantations flew back and forth between the fairies. Always, though, Emmeline was pushed farther and farther off the strand, until she stood up to her waist in the waves. Each of Manon's chants seemed to weigh on me, as if rocks were being piled atop my shoulders. And with each intonation, the waves rose a little higher on our tiny island.

Finally Luna could bear it no longer. She grabbed Leander's arm. "Do something!" she commanded him. "This is all your fault, you wretched imp! If you hadn't started it all by spurning Manon—"

His composure was shaken. "Don't you think I know that?" he said. "But I cannot cast spells—I am not a fairy. My speed through air and water will not help here. There is nothing I can do."

"If you love her, do something," Luna repeated hotly.

"You must!" Symon urged, and I gave him a grateful look. "Aurora is your niece! You can't just let Manon have her!"

My uncle's calm, impassive face changed then. For just a moment, his features showed a trace of what the years had cost him—losing his family, losing his human self. There was an almost unbearable sadness in his eyes.

"Yes. You are quite right." Prince Leander squared his shoulders and stood straighter. For the first time, I could see in him a little of the young prince as Mama had described him, ardent and strong. He stepped between the two fairies.

Manon had just spoken, and the strength of her spell sent him reeling to his knees. He struggled up and moved toward her, bent at the middle as if he were pushing against a great wind. He reached out, the strain of the movement showing in his face. When it seemed that he was about to grab Manon and choke her, she laughed, and his arms dropped lifelessly to his sides.

"Prince Leander to the rescue!" she scoffed. "You silly creature, what do you think to do against me? I can finish you with a flick of my wrist." And she flicked her hand, sending Leander sprawling on the wet sand.

"No!" cried Emmeline, trying to pull herself out of the water. "This is between us, Manon! It is not about Leander."

"Of course it is about Leander," Manon retorted. "It was always about Leander. You took him from me when he was mine—mine!" I could hardly bear to listen and watch. Emmeline had spoken the truth. Manon was mad, utterly mad.

"Please, do not destroy him," Emmeline pleaded.

Manon smiled at her, most dreadfully. "Yes, Cousin, what a waste that would be! Since you ask so nicely, I will not destroy him. Instead, I believe I will take him back."

Standing knee-deep in the seawater, Emmeline covered her mouth with her hand in horror.

"Do you release him, Emmeline? Will you give him back to me?"

There was a moment of silence, and then Emmeline said, in a shaking voice, "Yes. I do release him. You are free to go with Manon, Leander."

Leander got to his feet slowly and methodically began brushing the sand from his clothes. "But I was always free to go," he said, unflustered. "I am with you because I love you, Emmeline."

"Then I give you a choice," Manon snarled, her tone ferocious. "You may come with me and stay a lutin, or become human again, and grow old like a man, and die."

Emmeline wailed then, a sound of utter despair. I grabbed Symon's hand hard enough to make him wince. I was sure that Prince Leander would never choose to become old and ugly and to die, when he could be immortal.

Leander bent a little to adjust his tunic. I couldn't see his face, so I didn't know what the words he spoke cost him, but his voice was tranquil. "Why, that is no choice at all," he said. "I choose life and Emmeline, not the living death that eternity with you would force me to endure."

Perhaps he could have put it more diplomatically. His reply stunned me, and I realized that he was stronger than he seemed. He had courage—and he truly loved Emmeline.

His words enraged Manon. As her anger intensified, the wind that blew across the strand gusted, whipping the waves higher. Now the land that we stood on was just a strip of sand, and the dark water lapped at our feet.

"So be it!" Manon cried, pointing at Prince Leander. I feared he would immediately grow ancient and wizened and wither before our eyes, but he didn't change visibly. A great shudder shook his body, and then he was still.

Emmeline splashed over to him, and he put his arms around her. I saw Manon flinch. And then she turned once more to me.

"I shall not let you off so easily, my dear," she said in a voice of deceptive sweetness.

Symon stepped bravely in front of me, but again Manon flicked her wrist, and he sailed through the air, landing with a splash a few yards away. He scrambled to his feet, but before he could get back to my side, Luna leaped forward.

"You must curse me instead," she said firmly.

Manon paused. It was clear that she had not been expecting this.

"Why would I want to bother with you?" she asked with real curiosity.

"My sister shouldn't have to sleep for a century,"

Luna said. "I'm the one who should be punished. She's done nothing wrong—never in her entire life! Not like me—I've lied, and deceived, and destroyed things, and hurt people. It's my fault that she pricked her finger at all. I deserve the curse, not Aurora."

The wind died into a great silence. I put my hand on Luna's shoulder, sending her all the love and strength I could through my touch. I looked at Manon. Her face was thoughtful.

"Do you truly believe that you deserve it?" she asked Luna.

"Yes, I do," she replied without hesitation.

Manon shook her head and laughed. "Foolish girl," she said with contempt. "You are not what you think you are, nor is your sister. And the spell is already cast. It was settled the moment I cursed Aurora as an infant. There is no way to change it from one sister to the other, even if I desired it."

I gave Luna's shoulder a loving squeeze, then released her. I pushed her aside and stood alone to face Manon. Out of the corner of my eye, I saw Luna splashing through the rising water to Emmeline, who stood motionless beside Prince Leander, her face grief-stricken.

"You must help Aurora!" Luna begged Emmeline. Her voice sounded faint and faraway to me. "Can't you amend the curse? You did it once. You must alter it, shorten it—the way you did before. Not death for Mama, but a hundred years of sleep. Not a hundred years of sleep for Aurora, but . . ."

"Alter it?" Emmeline repeated uncertainly. "I'm not sure. . . ." Then her tone changed. "There is something—oh, Luna! Tell me, quickly, when is your sister's birthday?"

"It's . . . September twentieth," Luna answered, bewildered. I heard their words as if from a great distance. They had no meaning to me. I was beginning to fade.

At that moment, Manon spoke. "Come here, Princess," she said in a strangely tender voice. She reached out her hand and touched me, ever so gently, on the cheek. With her touch, Sleep came out from its hiding place, and the temptation that I had battled for so long grew too strong to resist.

It felt as I had always imagined death would feel—a slow, dizzying fall into a void. It was a little like being back in the whirlpool. I could not scream or even speak. I saw those I loved as I spun—Luna, shocked and horrified; Emmeline, turning to hide her face in Leander's shoulder. And Symon, his expression one of deepest sorrow. *I will miss you,* I thought as blackness enfolded me. *Do not forget me!*

17

Of a Dreamer's Destination

I had a dream.

In my dream, I heard a terrible noise and the crackle and hiss of flames. I felt cold water and salt spray, and then I was back in the *Cateline*, speeding across the sea. But it couldn't be the *Cateline*, for I knew the little boat had been destroyed in the whirlpool. I lay with my head in my sister's lap, feeling her familiar touch on my brow.

I heard Luna ask, "Will she wake?" She asked it over and over, her tone insistent and desperate. Emmeline's reply was always the same: "I believe she will, darling."

I felt the sun on my face, and then it was gone. This happened three times. Once there was an extraordinary splash and a wave that nearly capsized us. Luna's voice came faintly to me: "A whale!" she cried. "Oh, look at its eye!" I struggled to open my own eyes to see the marvel, but I could not.

Time passed in my dream, and the boat scraped on sand. Waves broke on a shore, and gulls called overhead. There were people all around, their voices rising and falling. At first they cried out in fear, but Symon spoke to them. He told them who we were; he convinced them that we were not pirates or brigands. I heard a family offer us their home, the father's voice gruff, the mother's soft and gentle, and I felt myself lifted and carried. They placed me on a scratchy mattress in a warm room. There was a delicious smell of stewed meat, and my mouth watered.

"Why does she sleep so soundly?" a little girl asked, but her mother hushed her.

"She is enchanted," I heard Luna reply.

"Will she ever wake?" another girl inquired.

"Of course she will," Luna said.

"Why do you wear boys' clothes?" one of them asked next.

"Child, don't be rude!" the same woman exclaimed.

"No, it's all right," Luna assured her. "I wear them

because I am a sailor, and you can't sail in skirts."

"And is that why your hair is short?" asked the girl.

"My hair is short because I like it that way," Luna told her. I wanted to smile, for Luna sounded so much like herself. But I could not make my muscles move, even my lips.

"Mama!" said the girl. "I am going to cut off all my hair and wear boys' clothes, just like Princess Luna!"

"You most certainly are not," the mother said sternly. She sent the children out to play, and I thought, *How I wish that I could see these people!* But I knew that they would die long before I woke.

There were no voices for a time, though I could hear and smell things I had never truly noticed before. The breeze shushed through the window of the room, bringing the scent of wisteria with it. The fire crackled and smoked on the hearth. And then I heard my father whisper.

"Where is your sister?"

"She is asleep, over there," Luna said. "But she will wake! She will wake, Papa."

And next came Mama, murmuring, "Aurora, dearest." Her voice caught on a sob. Her skirts rustled as she moved to where I lay, and I breathed in the spice-and-rose scent she always wore. I felt her gentle hand on my forehead, smoothing back my hair.

"My sweet child," she said softly.

Then Leander spoke. I couldn't hear what he said, but Mama cried out, "Oh, Brother, can it be you?" I struggled to break through to wakefulness, for I longed to see Mama and Leander reunited.

"Sleep, darling," Mama said to me then, her voice soothing. "Everything will be well. Sleep now."

And with that, something . . . changed. All at once Sleep, which had until now been a force that terrified and repelled me, softened and altered. Invisible arms reached out and cradled me. They were like my parents' arms, strong and protective. I sank into them gratefully and gave myself up to oblivion at last. I could see nothing, hear nothing. All was calm and quiet and dark.

18

Of a Welcome Wakefulness

I opened my eyes to daylight. I was lying down; I could feel a soft mattress beneath me, a coverlet atop me. When I focused my gaze upward, I saw that the ceiling above was undecorated, painted a soft blue, so I knew I was not in Emmeline's house. Then I remembered that her house—and the whole island—had dissolved under Manon's power. I remembered everything, and tears came to my eyes.

I turned my head and saw the window of my bedchamber at home. I was home. Castle Armelle still stood, even after a hundred years! I struggled to raise myself a bit, feeling very weak and shaky. Not much had changed, it seemed. My chair and love seat, my dressing table, the flowered rug on the floor beside my bed, all still remained. Even the bed hangings looked as fresh as when I had last awakened here, a century before. I was glad that everything had been kept the same.

The chamber door opened, and I braced myself. A servant I had never met would come in, or a relative three generations or more removed from my beloved family. I squeezed my eyes closed, willing myself to endure whatever anguish the visitor would bring.

"Oh, Sister, you're awake!" a familiar-sounding voice cried. My eyes flew open, and I saw Luna standing over me. She leaped onto the bed and hugged and kissed me, again and again, as I lay stunned and motionless.

This could not be Luna, I reasoned. It must be Luna's great-granddaughter. Or great-great-granddaughter. I was amazed at how much she looked like my sister, though I thought that her nose might be a little longer, her tawny eyes a little lighter in color. Even her short curls were similar. Perhaps, I thought, Luna's ridiculous haircut had spawned a new style that had persisted through the ages.

"Who . . . ?" was all I could manage, my long-unused voice coming out in a rasp.

"Don't try to speak, Aurora!" the girl exclaimed,

bouncing wildly on my bed. "I cannot believe it worked! We didn't know for sure—though Emmeline promised us—but it was hard to have faith in her, you know. She's really not very reliable with her magic. But she did this right. Oh, I must tell Mama and Papa!" She jumped off the bed and headed for the door.

"Wait," I croaked. "How . . . ?"

The girl turned back. "That's right," she said in a voice full of wonder. "I forgot that you didn't know."

"Know . . . what?"

"That Emmeline amended the curse. That you have not slept for a hundred years, but only for two months."

I stared at her, disbelieving.

"She changed it, Aurora, just as she did for Mama. From one hundred years to the end of your twelfth year."

I was speechless, and as I gazed at the girl she was transformed before my eyes. Why, of course that was Luna's own upturned nose, her warm smile! This was not Luna's great-great-granddaughter, but my own sweet sister. And with that realization, I burst into tears.

Luna became frantic. "Oh no, no, please don't cry! Oh, Sister, I'm sorry, it's all too much. . . . Let me get Mama and Papa."

I nodded, weeping, and she ran off, calling for our

parents. They could not have been far away, for they came into my room almost at once. At the sight of their dear faces, worn with worry and care, I cried even harder.

Mama rushed to me and took me in her arms, and I remembered the feeling of Sleep's embrace as I surrendered. I had thought then that I would never see Mama again—yet here she was, only two months older! Then Papa hugged me, whispering, "Hello, Daughter!" He stood and blew his nose in a snow-white handkerchief and handed another one to me, and I wiped my eyes.

Mama sat beside me on the bed and stroked my brow. "We have been attending to you each day, Aurora, brushing your hair so it did not tangle and making sure you were comfortable in every way. It was all that we could do. . . . Oh, dearest, the waiting has been agony!"

"Poor Mama," I murmured, patting her hand. "You must have taken very good care of me. I feel well enough—rested, at last! But I think I am very weak."

"You've been lying down for two months," Luna pointed out. "But once you are up, I'm sure you'll get your strength back quickly. I'll help."

I smiled at her. There was a knock at the door, and Luna ran to open it. In came Emmeline, her face beaming, and behind her was Prince Leander.

"I am awake, Godmother," I said happily.

"So I see, darling. Good for you!" she exclaimed. "Oh, I am so very glad it worked!"

Mama gasped. "Emmeline, you promised it would work!"

Emmeline reddened. "I was fairly certain," she said, looking at the floor.

Mama stood, putting a delicate hand to her throat. "Fairly? If I had known it might fail . . ."

"But it did not fail," Prince Leander cut in easily. "All is well, Sister."

I looked at the prince—my uncle!—as he hugged Mama to him. They were together at last, after a hundred years and more. Mama looked happier than I could ever remember her, her cheeks flushed with pink.

Then I recalled what had happened on the island. Leander's face was no longer perfect; a few lines marred the smoothness of his skin. "Are you . . . ," I began, but I could think of no way to ask gracefully what I wanted to know. Luckily, Luna had no qualms.

"Uncle Leander is a human now," she told me, perching beside me again. "Do you remember that? He chose to be one—it was very noble."

"Very romantic," I said, and Emmeline smiled.

"Yes, both romantic and noble," she agreed.

"Leander insists that he will remain young in spirit, even as his body ages. And I will give up my vanity and age with him, as much as I can." She reached for Leander's hand and squeezed it. I was close enough to see the sadness in her eyes, though, and my heart ached for her. How dreadful it would be for her to have to watch her beloved die, while she lived on and on!

But Emmeline could not stay unhappy for long. Her face grew merry again, and she said, "But he will always be the handsomest man in the world, even when he is old and gray. And he will never be nearly as old as I!"

At this, Leander laughed. It was a completely human laugh, joyous and sorrowful at the same time.

"But where is Master Julien? Surely he is not in the dungeon, is he? And Symon—is he here?" I inquired in what I hoped was a nonchalant voice.

"Our tutor is busy doing what he does best—teaching," Luna said.

"Oh, has he found another position?" I asked.

Luna grinned at me. "No indeed," she said gleefully. "He's teaching Symon geography. And cartography. And astronomy, and mathematics as well. It's quite a fascinating course of learning. I've been studying with them."

"But why?"

"Symon wants to give up fishing for exploring, and

Papa promised to be his patron," Luna explained. "First, though, Symon must learn to sail a ship big enough for an expedition. A batteau could not make such a journey." She dropped her voice to a whisper and said, into my ear, "I plan to go with him. It will take me years to convince Mama and Papa, but I'll do it. I'll see the world!"

"How remarkable!" I said softly. It seemed that things had not stayed the same during my long sleep after all. I thought of what I had said, teasingly, to Symon about raising a fortune and calling on me when we were grown, and I smiled a little to myself.

"I want to get up," I announced.

"Oh, dearest, should you?" Mama asked anxiously.

"Of course she should!" Luna said. She put an arm around me, and together we struggled until I could swing my legs over the side of the bed. I had a moment of dizziness sitting up, but then the room righted itself. Luna helped me into an embroidered robe and slippers, and I stood unsteadily. Then, with Luna's support, I walked over to my love seat and sat. My limbs trembled from the effort of walking, and my stomach growled loudly.

"Why, I'm starving," I said.

"Jacquelle!" Mama called, and the maid entered the room immediately. She had obviously been listening just outside the door. "Bring tea and toast for Princess Aurora."

"Mama, I haven't eaten since July!" I exclaimed. "Please, Jacquelle, bring sausages! Bring cheese crepes, and cocoa. And a dish of berries and cream." My mouth watered just to say the words.

"Yes, Your Highness." Jacquelle bobbed in a curtsy. "It's very good to see you awake, Your Highness!"

"Thank you," I said, smiling hugely. My smile stayed in place as I looked around at all my family: Mama, Papa, Emmeline, Uncle Leander, and Luna—Luna, who had tried so hard to save me.

"Do Mama and Papa know everything that happened?" I asked my sister. "Do they know how you tried to get Manon to curse you instead of me?"

"I told them," Emmeline said. "Luna would not say a word about it when we came back. But you are the one who does not know the whole story, my dear. You do not know that it was Luna's idea that saved you. You do not know how Manon perished."

"Manon is gone? Gone for good? Oh, what happened?" I cried.

"I'll tell," Luna said. "I think I can talk about it now."

"Yes, you tell," I agreed, stroking her bouncy curls.

"Well," Luna began, "at the moment Manon touched you, Emmeline spoke. 'I amend your curse!' she said. 'Aurora shall not sleep for a hundred years. Instead, I say that she will sleep only until the end of the year in which the curse took hold. She will wake at the same moment she was born—on September twentieth, her thirteenth birthday!'"

"Oh," I said in wonder. "How clever, Godmother!"

"It was not my idea," Emmeline admitted. "I had spent my time trying to strengthen my magic, for I wanted to do away with Manon's spell altogether. But in the end, I didn't have the power. It was only when Luna urged me that I realized that altering the curse might work. Manon was not expecting me to do it a second time—she was entirely absorbed by her desire for revenge."

"She underestimated you, my love," Leander said warmly, and Emmeline smiled her beautiful smile at him.

"Manon couldn't bear it," Luna went on. "I was standing near her, and Symon pulled me away. It was a good thing he did! Oh, you've never imagined anything like it. She was so angry that she couldn't speak. She quivered and sputtered, and her hair lifted and crackled as if it were filled with lightning. I was sure that she would turn on us and change us into some dreadful creatures, or into rocks, or simply drown us in the seawater." Luna winced at the memory, and I took her hand.

"But instead, as we watched, she got redder and

redder until she was practically purple. Then she began to swell like a bullfrog. Her face puffed up, and the buttons popped off her dress. She grew enormous, all swollen and plum-colored. I was so frightened. . . ." Her voice trailed off shakily. We waited in silence for a moment, but Luna couldn't go on.

Emmeline took over the story. "It seemed as though she couldn't possibly expand any further. Then all at once there was a tremendous booming explosion. It was like a thunderclap. Right before our eyes she burst into flame."

I gasped and squeezed Luna's hand. "I screamed," Luna said in a low voice. "We all screamed, I think. It was the most awful thing I'd ever seen. The blaze burned so fast! It was incredibly hot. In just a minute, she was utterly consumed. It looked like she still stood before us, but it was only her shape, outlined in ashes. There was a little puff of wind, and the ashes crumbled to the surface of the sea, hissing. Manon was there, and then she was gone. There was no trace of her left at all."

"I've never heard of such a thing!" I said, appalled.

"Spontaneous combustion, Master Julien called it when we told him," Luna explained. "He'd thought it happened only in books. I've never even dreamed of anything so frightful." She grimaced and closed her eyes, remembering.

"Manon had lived with her jealousy and her fury for so long that she could no longer hold it inside," Emmeline told me. "When she knew she'd lost Leander for good, when I bested her by changing the curse a second time—her hatred grew too big to contain. It destroyed her."

I shuddered. "I'm glad she is gone," I said fiercely to Luna. "You were so brave, Sister!"

Luna's eyes were filled with tears. "I haven't been able to speak of it before," she confessed. "I've had nightmares nearly every night since it happened."

"But now the nightmare is over," I said softly, hugging her.

She leaned into me, gulping back a sob, and whispered, "Yes, the nightmare is over at last!"

Of Sisters
Side by Side

A knock sounded at the door, and Cook entered with a covered tray. "Happy birthday, Your Highness!" she cried, laughing with pleasure as I dug into the food. "I'm making the biggest, most beautiful birthday cake you have ever seen!"

Never had a sausage tasted so wonderful, nor a berry so sweet and juicy. I could not stop eating. I chewed and swallowed as quickly as I could. "How odd, that it should be September, and my birthday," I said as soon as my mouth was empty.

"You are thirteen years old today," Mama said fondly. "Do not eat so fast, dearest—it is not seemly, and you will belch." It was what Mama always said, and as always, it made Luna laugh.

When I finished, I walked around the room slowly, testing my strength. My terrible exhaustion was gone at last, and the food had given me new energy.

Luna walked with me, supporting me when I needed help, and when we were on the opposite side of the room from Mama and Papa, she spoke in a low voice. "Before she . . . died, Manon said something to me. Something strange."

"What was it?" I asked.

"She said, 'You are not what you think you are, nor is your sister.' She called me foolish. What do you think she meant? I can't stop wondering about it."

I remembered the moment on the sandbar when Manon had uttered those words. "I think she spoke the truth," I said. "She saw that you believed yourself to be a bad person, with no good in you. And somehow she knew how good I'd always thought myself. But we were both wrong."

Luna looked bewildered. "But you *are* good," she said uncertainly.

"I'm vain, and I'm terribly timid," I told her. "And you're brave and loving and generous. We're both a mixture, not one extreme or the other."

"You're not timid anymore," Luna pointed out. "A timid girl wouldn't have jumped on that quicksand to save me. Or held on to the sail ropes when the dragon came."

"Well," I said, "maybe I'm not quite so timid as I was."

"And am I really all those things?" Luna asked, her eyes shining.

"Truly," I assured her. When her grin became almost too big for her face, I added, "And a dreadful pest, of course." She pinched me, and I yelped.

The door opened again then, and at last Master Julien and Symon entered. In three quick strides Symon was at my side, and my heart quickened.

"Oh, Aurora," he said breathlessly, and stopped. He was quite unable to go on. I glanced quickly at Mama and Papa, worried that this display of affection might anger them, but they didn't seem disturbed.

Luna read my thoughts. "They've seen Symon's devotion to you," she whispered to me. "He's spent hours at your side every day. They know what he did for us, and they're truly pleased and grateful."

I looked at Symon's sun-browned face, his wild hair and bright eyes, and opened my mouth to speak. I wasn't at all sure what I would say, but I wanted him to know how very much he had come to mean to me.

Instead, I belched.

Luna let out a shriek of laughter, and all the tension went out of the room. Symon laughed too, and Leander and Emmeline had tears running down their faces. Mama was horrified, of course, and my own cheeks were hot, but I had to smile and finally to join in the laughter.

"Oh, romance!" Luna moaned, holding her stomach. I smacked her—but lightly.

The moment for declarations had passed, and I needed to sit down again. I took Symon by the hand and pulled him to the love seat. "You must tell me," I said. "How did we get back?"

"We sailed in Manon's boat," he said.

"In the black-sailed boat?" I asked, remembering my hazy half dream.

"Yes, to the town of Deleau," he replied. "It is a tiny fishing village. The people were terrified of us."

"I dreamed that," I said in wonder. "There was a family, wasn't there? Some children . . ."

"That's right!" Luna broke in, eavesdropping. "The Michels, and their twin daughters. They were very kind to us and sent for Mama and Papa. But you were asleep; how did you know?"

I shook my head. "I was asleep, but not asleep. It was the strangest thing."

"Papa gave the Michels a gold coin for helping us,"

Luna said. "And he has met Madame Mathilde and Albert, who aided us in Vittray. They sent word to Mama and Papa that we were well, as they promised. Papa has vowed that the palace would buy all of Albert's catch for as long as he fished, to thank him."

"And he pledged to give Albert a new mast," Symon added. I remembered—it had been Albert's extra, unfinished mast with the pine pitch that ended up saving us from Melusine.

"And then," Luna went on, "we rode home from Deleau, and everyone gathered along the way to cheer and salute us. It was quite wonderful. You were in the carriage with Mama, but I was on horseback. You would have liked it if you'd ridden with us."

"Oh, I don't think I would have—all those strangers!" I protested. I was too used to solitude and seclusion.

"They are your people," Symon pointed out. "You'll be their queen someday. You must learn to love them."

I thought about how I had felt in the Michels' house in my half sleep, how I had longed to see them and get to know them. Now I had been given a chance to do that.

"You're right," I said to Symon. "I've been shut up too long. I think that I slept even when I was awake." Luna looked quizzical at my words, but before she could jump in with questions, I heard an odd noise. It sounded like many voices, and music too.

"What is that?" I asked.

Luna listened for a moment. "It's the people of Vittray," she replied.

"What do you mean?"

"They came to see you wake up, and to celebrate your birthday," Luna said. "Papa has promised them birthday cake. In the meantime, he's given them bread and cheese and our best cider, and sent musicians to entertain them."

"But . . . ," I said hesitantly, still afraid, "I don't know them."

"Ah, but they know you!" Luna said. "They've all heard your story. And they know me—I've been at every market day since we came back, and in every single shop in town!"

I stared at my sister. "Have you? You're so much bolder than I, Luna."

"You'll come too, now that you're awake," Luna said with certainty. "We're no longer locked away, Sister. We have nothing more to fear."

"That is so," I said wonderingly. I knew I didn't want to travel the world on a ship, like Luna. What I wanted was much, much smaller, but it was still so much more than what I'd had before. I wanted to go out among Papa's subjects—my subjects, one day—and get to know them.

"If they're here to celebrate my birthday," I said

resolutely, "then I should go out to them."

"Oh, is that wise?" Mama fretted.

I repeated Luna's words. "We have nothing more to fear."

Then I smiled at my sister. "And you must come too, Luna! For we are celebrating your courage as much as my awakening. And Symon's valor as well. And Emmeline's magic, and Leander's great sacrifice. We'll celebrate it all!"

"But you are not dressed, dearest," Mama pointed out. "And your hair is not done!"

I looked down at my robe and nightdress and then at Luna, and she and I grinned at each other. "The people will simply have to take me as I am," I said.

And with a strength in my step that I had never felt, not even before the fateful day I pricked my finger, I led the others out of my bedchamber. They followed me down the hall to the balcony that overlooked the courtyard, and I threw open the doors.

Luna and I walked out onto the balcony, hands clasped together. The September sun shone down brightly. Below us, the people clustered on the greensward beyond the gravel drive, drinking cider and eating. The sounds of lute and drum and pipe filled the air, and children twirled in a delighted dance around the musicians.

Then someone looked up and noticed us and pulled on another's cloak, and they pointed and spoke to others. Everyone began to move toward the palace. The music stopped, and gradually the throng grew quiet, their eager faces upturned. I saw Madame Mathilde and Albert in front of the crowd, their family beside them.

Luna poked me. "There are the Michels!" she whispered. Behind Madame Mathilde was a family of four, a tall, skinny man, his tiny wife, and two identical little girls, who swung on their father's hands. I waved shyly at them, and a roar went up from the waiting assembly. I was astounded.

Papa and Mama came out onto the balcony, and the crowd cheered all the more. Then Papa held up a hand, and they quieted.

"My people," Papa proclaimed, "you have been gracious and loyal, and we thank you for your good thoughts and your support in this difficult time." Again the crowd cheered. "As you can see, my daughter has awakened, and both of our beloved girls are here beside us, well and happy." The people shouted their approval.

"My daughters' courage, and the courage of their friends, has brought them safely through their adventures." Papa motioned, and Symon, looking abashed, joined us to wild cheers.

Papa stepped back then, and at the same moment Luna and I turned to each other. I threw my arms around her and hugged her as hard as I could. Once more the crowd roared. The music started up, and as a joyful dance began below us, Cook and Jacquelle came out to the greensward pushing a tray on wheels. Atop it was a gigantic cake, tier upon tier of white-frosted layers decorated with whorls of colored icing and flowers as vivid as those in Emmeline's garden.

"It's your birthday cake!" Luna cried, clapping her hands. "Oh, let's have some!"

"I must go down," I said to Papa, and he replied, "Yes, go!" Even Mama nodded.

Then, still in my dressing gown with my hair unbrushed, I turned and sped through the hallway. Luna was just behind me and Symon followed, while our parents, Emmeline, Uncle Leander, and Master Julien watched. Hungry for cake and dancing and people and life, I flew down the stairs and into the courtyard, wide awake and ready to join the revelry.